THE INQUISITOR'S DIARY

a novel by
JEFFREY LEWIS

First published in 2013 by Haus Publishing Limited

HAUS PUBLISHING LTD.
70 Cadogan Place, London SW1X 9AH
www.hauspublishing.com

Copyright © Jeffrey Lewis 2013

Print ISBN 978-1-908323-31-6
ebook ISBN 978-1-908323-32-3

Typeset in Garamond by MacGuru Ltd
info@macguru.org.uk

Printed and bound by CPI Group (UK) Ltd, Croydon, CR0 4YY

A CIP catalogue for this book is available from the British Library

The Inquisitor's Diary

If we want to have a love which will protect the soul from wounds, we must love something other than God.

– Simone Weil

THE JOURNEY

Entries from 11 April to 26 November 1649

What a display! What a magnificent demonstration of our Holy
Faith which in a mere one hundred years has transformed a land
previously drenched in the sins of human sacrifice and pagan
orgy into a place of our Lord's most beneficent will! Dear God,
may You forgive my pride in this achievement. Yet I feel it would
perhaps be a greater evil to let this historic event go unpraised.
May peace and goodwill be upon Mexico! May peace and goodwill extend to the farthest reaches of our Hispanic Majesty's
dominions!

In honor of this day, I do not merely turn a page, I commence
an entirely new journal. This lovely volume of Moroccan calf
that Fray Sebastian was kind enough to bring me on his recent
arrival from Seville has found an unexpectedly pregnant occasion for its baptism. I thank you, Fray Sebastian, with open heart

and hand, and I hope this re-dedication of my efforts to record one sinner's life and quest will prove justification for your generosity. And your good taste, I might add. No leather is more suitable than Moroccan calf. Our Lord works in mysterious ways, granting gifts of skill even to the most fallen of his human flock. The Moor, benighted as he is in matters of the spirit, nonetheless knows his way around a cow's exterior.

Today we have witnessed in the City of Mexico a public Act of Faith scarcely to be outdone in Toledo or Cordoba. I shall refer to the figures, and may my heart be free from cruelty in so doing. One hundred and nine convicts, fourteen penitent, seventeen reconciled, sixty-five relaxed in effigy, thirteen relaxed in person. I have heard that for fifty leagues around the city, Spanish and natives alike left their houses to be present. From the Palace of our Holy Office to the Plazuela del Volador, one could walk on the shoulders of the faithful, feet never once touching the paving stones. Carriages of every luxurious appointment lined the side streets, rendered useless by the throngs. The mood everywhere, amidst every class, was expectant and celebratory.

And then came the procession of the convicted, in their garments of flames and tears. Of the entire proceeding it was this moment that most deeply engaged my soul. The crowds taunted and jeered, eager for that spectacle of death that must doubtless confirm their own salvation, but I was never so certain. My prayers redoubled in favor of last-minute conversions. Here at last, in a setting not unlike Your Son's own last journey, would not one or two souls see the blessed light of truth?

My prayers, or I should say, ours, for I make no claim to have been the only prayerful man in attendance, You answered beyond all hope or expectation. Of the thirteen *relajados,* twelve repented on way to the *quemadero.* What sinful soul could imagine it? Twelve of thirteen knelt and kissed the cross!

In consideration of the humility and wisdom of their acts, while yet recognizing their tardiness and the possibility of fraud which the situation allowed, our Holy Office, striving to be mindful of mercy, at once recommended to the secular authority that in each of their cases the garrote precede the stake.

Only one man was burned alive today. So wanton and perverse was this thick-necked soul, so tightly held in Satan's embrace, that I shall not even dignify his cursed name by writing it. A Franciscan well known to me, an excellent and just man, Fray Miguel de Castro, trailed the wretch on a mule the entire route to the Plazuela del Volador, in hopes of hearing any word of contrition. Instead what he heard was a kind of gibberish, which Fray Miguel believed to be Hebraic. I cannot confirm nor disprove that such was the case. But all in earshot could hear the damned one's perfectly pitched Spanish as he stood in the *quemadero*'s flames. A gag had been placed round his mouth to forbid his blasphemies, but he bit through the gag and shouted, 'Throw more wood on the fire, you wretches, for I am paying for this!' It is true what they say of the Jew, that to the last he thinks of money. The crowd, of course, loved it.

Everything went badly. I am disgusted with myself, first for having walked into a trap that I might have foreseen, and second for caring so much about having done so. Lord Jesus forgive me my anger, my disappointment, my self-pity. I shall strive, with Your grace, to be a better man than I am. But today I see all too clearly that I am wretched.

My appointment with the Inquisitor General was this afternoon. It appeared to go well from the outset. He offered me sherry and we chatted amiably about his new cook, a native who has arrived from the southern mountains with an extraordinary secret recipe for sweetening and then curing *cacao*, which the Inquisitor General promised to invite me soon to sample. He complimented me for the exactitude of my reasoning in the Flores case. I suppose I should have been on my guard just then, but, as You who are closer to me than my own hand know infinitely better than I, a man is never so exposed as when he has just been praised. I took what I thought was the opportunity to press my case for a transfer to Spain. I presented my arguments, which I had been accruing and polishing so eagerly in my head for the past months – my lack of previous transfers, how the Tribunal here might in subsequent years benefit from my exposure to proceedings at the *Suprema*, and so on. I reminded him of the forthcoming visit of the *Suprema*'s Holy Emissary and entreated him to urge my case with his Eminence. But I was caught entirely short.

The Inquisitor General took my desire to be away and turned it back on me. He said, 'So! You're bored! You're primed for an adventure! Well, I have just the assignment for you then!'

'What is that, sir?' I asked.

'I've recently been persuaded,' he began, 'that we have a growing problem on our northern frontiers. It is not the natives themselves, God's blessing on them. They of course relapse into superstition and witchcraft as if it were their birthright, which in a sense we must admit it is. We can deal with relapses. They are good-hearted souls and they come back to us, as soon as they are persuaded of their erroneous ways and the power of our Savior's forgiving love. No, what I'm hearing about are Europeans. Must I spell this out? The natives will listen to Europeans who fill their ears with heresy just as readily as they will listen to us. This is so, because, through us, they have come to trust what the white man avows. We must not allow the goodwill we have earned through a century's cultivation to be stolen from us by counterfeiters, Portuguese, even Protestants.'

The Inquisitor General sipped his sherry, his narrowed eyes scrutinizing me over his glass, as if to further propel the direction of his thought.

'Are there reports of Protestants proselytizing on our northern frontiers?' I asked.

'Not Protestants. Not yet.'

'But Portuguese?'

'Portuguese, yes.'

'Proselytizing?'

The Inquisitor General grew impatient with me. He put down his sherry. 'I am not in the dock, am I, counselor?'

'No, sir. I only ask because the Portuguese, as you say, are not known as proselytizers, and moreover we have made previous sweeps of the frontiers with only the sparsest of results. May I ask, sir, who introduced these suspicions to you?'

'Does that truly matter, Fray Alonso?'

'Yes, of course, if it's Fray Luis I have a right to know as much.'

'Fray Luis is hardly a fantasist.'

'But did he propose me for the job as well?'

'He bears you no animosity, you know.'

'Animosity? Sir…' I struggled with an outbreak of my least worthy feelings. I forbore calling our Tribunal's treasurer the various animal names that in my moment of anger I felt bore closest resemblance to his soul. 'Perhaps he has no ill feelings for me…'

'Quite the contrary. He respects you as a rock of tradition, of sound practice, of discipline…'

'In other words, a prig. Surely it cannot escape your observation, sir, that Fray Luis has certain ambitions which lead him, at times, sir, to seek, how shall I put it… to perhaps make it more difficult, rather than less so, for his colleagues' virtues to be seen?'

The Inquisitor General had had enough of my impertinence. 'You are accusing Fray Luis of sending you on a wild goose chase? If anyone is sending you on a wild goose chase, Fray Alonso, it is I, not Fray Luis! Do you imagine I can be so easily manipulated? Do you imagine Fray Luis has such influence?'

But it was Fray Luis, I was sure of it, who anyway had put it in the Inquisitor General's head. Or perhaps it was not even a wild goose chase he had in mind. Perhaps – I would not put it past him – Fray Luis implied to the Inquisitor General that there were rich confiscations to be found in the north. A corruption I cannot abide, yet a question I cannot avoid, given Fray Luis's fiscal role and the deference the Inquisitor General shows him in all matters budgetary. And now I shall not be going to Spain, which fired my imagination for so many years. I shall not even have the chance to put my case to the *Suprema*'s emissary, for I will be leagues and leagues away by the time of his arrival.

How I've dreamed of Seville! Of the afternoon light on the walls of Avila! Is it a sin to seek those places that our Holy Faith has beautified? Dear God, may my motives be only those of a pilgrim, may sensuality play no part in my desire.

Yet I wonder if I shall see Spain in my lifetime. I am like a man born into exile. Exile is his natural state. And now I shall be further exiled, to the pitiless north, deprived even of the modest wonders and spiritual nourishments of our capital.

Well played, Fray Luis. Cunningly executed. The reformer! The man of the future! Bah. Forgive me, I pray, but I shall write it again. Bah! He despises me mostly because I so thoroughly see through him.

One touching note about our Inquisitor General. How delicate he is, how old-fashioned, when he speaks of *the Portuguese*. Why, dear God, does he not simply say Jews?

19 April

Blessed Savior who is the light of my day and my night, I give thanks to You for permitting me to understand, on reflection, the Inquisitor General's fears. It is not a question of confiscations. Of course not, not with him, even if Fray Luis has implied to him these might be ample. No, the Inquisitor General does not wish the native population to become infected, howsoever inadvertently. And it sometimes takes but a single match to light a conflagration. We have made a great triumph here in New Spain and we must not squander it. This, I must remind myself, is the great purpose You have given my being. This is the life work of all of us, and those who doubt it must wonder too if it is not Satan who has planted such doubts.

Nonetheless, I fear my next year will be wasted, amidst dessicated plants and snakes. And I am disappointed.

24 April

The final nail in the coffin of my hopes. Our esteemed treasurer's allocation! The amount of three thousand pesos, sufficient for a journey of 'a thousand leagues or a thousand days,' as they say. I would like to assure my dear colleagues, even our most precious dear Fray Luis, that I am not making a journey of a thousand days! They'll not be rid of me for that long!

More like a hundred. With God's help I will be home with my bagful of heretics in a hundred.

In the meantime, what choice have I but to begin preparations? Hires of the day: two muleteers. Tomorrow I shall interview porters. I will do myself a service by admitting to one and all that I know little about such journeys. I shall place myself in the hands of a provisioner. The Tribunal wishes me to go, the Tribunal will provide me the wherewithal to do so. Eggs, however! Is it a sin to wish for fresh eggs?

The most contradictory advice on the weather. 'Depart before May 1.' Of course, impossible. 'Depart before May 15.' Likely also impossible. 'But no matter what you do, there'll be no avoiding the hottest days of the desert.' 'But if you wait till winter, matters will be even worse.'

27 April

I ran into Fray Luis this morning, at the refectory of the Dominicans. Exuding solicitude, of course, and at the same time wishing me happy hunting and expatiating on the vital significance of my undertaking. Where do they breed such hypocrites? Most offensively, he took it upon himself to remind me of the Office's policy against harassing the native population. Well, good, I suppose – at least he takes me to be an ignorant fool, as well as everything else. From such underestimations, if

9

I may presume to hope that they are, some evil might one day befall him.

I am being uncharitable. Of course I am. I must be more charitable. I must not permit envy, choler, even my perceived injustice, to distort me.

I shall do exactly as I am chartered, as the Inquisitor General requests of me. As for Fray Luis, it is not mine to complain one jot. We all have our crosses. Dear Holy Father whose air we breathe, whose food we eat, I trust and pray that You will deal with Fray Luis as Your infinite wisdom and goodness deem proper.

Hired today, a native guide. Though they say the trail as far as Nuevo Leon is as obvious as your hand.

3 May

Tomorrow we shall depart. Six muleteers, four porters, a guide, a cook and myself. I have taken care that each porter and two of the muleteers are skilled in firearms.

A full day of prayers and blessings ahead of all of us. Even the mules get blessed. I should hope so. Nothing more crucial than that the mules be blessed.

En route
6 May

No more tedious a journey could have been conceived to teach man wariness of earthly seduction. We have entered upon the endless *altiplano*. Its apologists, our guide among them, tell me we are in years of drought. All I can see at every vista is unrelieved desiccation, every scrub plant starved of nourishment, starved of everything but the sun's relentless stare. One could almost wish for hostile Indians, if only to relieve the boredom.

14 June

By my best estimates it is just about now that the *Suprema*'s emissary should be arriving in the capital, inspecting our operations, having dinner with the Inquisitor General, and meeting with all the rest. When I am reminded, it causes me deep regret and considerable bitterness, which I confess I struggle, and fail, to subdue. I am here and he will be there, and there is no help for it.

17 June

Today I was informed that we had left New Spain and entered into the province of Nuevo Leon. How our esteemed guide was able to make this determination remains a mystery to me. Did the lizards change color on the border? He also suggested to me that we are now five days from Monterrey.

Monterrey
27 June

I note that my previous entry predicted a five day journey to Monterrey. The Sierra Madre begged to differ. Albeit tardily, we arrived today. I should remark regarding our journey to date, that it has been rather more taxing on our physiques than I cared to note while we were in transit. Now that we have arrived in 'safe harbor', so to speak, I may admit that the heat, the long marches, the poor sleep at night on account of lookouts for snakes and poisonous insects of every description, the climbs and descents, the exhaustion of our meat supply and our inability to fully replenish it with our guns, all made for a considerable trial. Of course, the natives bear up under all of this much better than myself or my Spanish colleagues. They accept the minimal as normal. I cannot help but admire this. How soft I am, how soft we Europeans are.

Dear Jesus, I should say my spirit suffered as well. Full of resentments, angers, urges to revenge myself for being put through these paces for reasons either corrupt or insensibly stupid. There were days when every step I took on the scorching earth was accompanied by some evil fancy of violence or cruelty. I pray to rediscover my less unworthy self in this, as it were, oasis.

It appears that the *custos* here in Monterrey, one Fray Donaldo, has arranged lodgings for us in an airy hostel overlooking a pleasant cow pond. Ah, a roof over our heads!

28 June

It does my soul no credit for there to be yet another churchman I find disagreeable. Doubtless it is a reflection of that old-fashionedness of which I am accused, which in my view is no more than an adherence to traditional norms of collegiality, sincerity and propriety, which others may have forgotten. Nonetheless I do not like this Fray Donaldo. Not one bit. It is true that he has lodged us, and more than adequately, and of course for this I am grateful. But he seems to resent my arrival here. Why, he asks, if he is *custos* for Nuevo Leon, has the Holy Office sent *me*? Does my mission suggest a dissatisfaction in the capital with the job he is doing? I try to impress upon him quite the contrary, that my role is no more than to see to it that he has all the assistance he needs in carrying out his mission. I try to suggest in tactful terms, terms such that he could not then turn against me, that my mission was by no means my idea and I would rather have spent a week in a ring with a famished bull than have embarked upon it.

But he is having none of it. He wishes to assure me that from the time of the Carvajals, fifty years ago, the New Christians, the judaizers, the *conversos* of Nuevo Leon have been dealt with. 'The Governor's family did burn for judaizing, for heresy, for heaven's sake,' he told me. Of course I do not need a history lesson from his like, I whom at headquarters they lightly mock as 'office historian' for my comprehensive recall of past cases. As for the Carvajals, I could recite him every detail of each family member's heresy. The same with the Mattos, the Vicentes, the Corderos, the Trinocos, the Sevillas, the Sobremontes. But what would be the point? Pride is my demon, I must not feed it inadvertently.

Instead I tried to suggest to Fray Donaldo that all I would like to do is review his records and perhaps copy a portion of them, so that on my return I might reassure the Holy Office that things are well in hand here. He answered back, 'My records are not all in one place. You've surprised me with this visit. You'll have to wait some days, I'm afraid.'

I said, 'Then we will wait.'

Perhaps he does not realize how much I will appreciate just such a respite.

The cathedral here is quite stunning, both in its height and in the harmony of its construction. The entire province, as we know, was built principally by *conversos* who were not permitted into New Spain. There must have been some men of earnest piety among them, or I do not believe they could have built such an exquisite structure.

This goes, dear Lord, to the heart of my concerns with some of my brethren. They do not give *any* New Christians the benefit of the doubt. All, in their suspicion, are relapsers, judaizers, heretics-in-waiting. I say to allow such suspicions to dominate one's reason is an insult to the power of our faith. Surely, many Jews came to the Church due not to fear alone, but to the infinite reach of Your love. We men of the Holy Office must never forget this. Our powers give us great responsibility. We must not exercise them cynically. We must be honest judges.

2 July

No heretics in Nuevo Leon. *Custos* Fray Donaldo has now presented me with records that I have no reason to doubt. He may bc peevish and impertinent, but such types of men as he tend to keep good records. I have copied down the relevant portions. We shall leave Monterrey, I'm mildly sorry to relate, either later tomorrow or the morning following. The route of trade goes north–northwest, largely following what are described to me as magnificent riverbeds and chasms of the three rivers, the Rio Grande, the Rio Bravo and the Rio del Norte, until we virtually reach our destination, the provincial outpost called *La Villa Real de la Santa Fé de San Francisco de Asis*. A bit of a mouthful, to be sure. I believe this portion of our journey may be, if no less harsh with us, nonetheless more pleasing to the eye.

En route
11 July

Hardly enough water in this muddy river to bathe in, and if you did bathe in it, I'd venture you would come out filthier than when you went in. No one, I should note, has thus far taken the plunge. Even the mules seem reluctant to drink in the puddles, which are like soupy red clay. And the heat is devastating. I have ordered a shortening of our marches. We proceed from dawn for three hours, then again for the three hours leading up to dusk. The remainder of the day we seek cover in whatever shade is available.

I am estimating we shall not see our destination until October.

3 August

We have reached the bend of the Rio Bravo. I regret to record that one of our porters, an Indian whose Christian name was Marcos, died of fevers last night. One of the mules was made to carry him these past days, which was hardly good for the mule, but my rule has been that no man shall be abandoned except if the circumstances overwhelmingly require it. We said prayers, I made a service, we buried him by the river under a cross of ironwood.

10 August

I note the hundredth day since our departure. And to think that I once scribbled in these very pages that we would be home in a hundred. The self-deluding drivel that I am capable of! Dear God, chastise me for my arrogance, my foolhardiness, my endless pride, so like a thousand-headed monster.

3 September

Today we encountered the first of the so-called *Pueblos*. The ingenuity of these constructions has caused me to reevaluate my opinion of native gifts. The more I see of these magnificent, tall habitations, so uniquely suited to the arid conditions of this country, the more I am convinced that these natives possess every aptitude and intelligence necessary for a full appreciation of our Holy Faith.

Yet at the same time I am continually reminded of the

doubtfulness of my own personal mission. Heretics on our northern frontier? As far as I have seen so far, there are not even any Christians on our northern frontier. Or not any European Christians, anyway. The occasional trader with his mule pack. The occasional mission man with his flock of Indians, as here at this *Pueblo.* Of course, I remind myself, all will be different when we reach the province's capital.

3 October

We followed a narrow riverine track for several hours, until, at mid-afternoon, Arroyo Ricardo halted our advance and brought me ahead with him, around a rocky outcrop. 'There!' He pointed in an easterly direction. 'Santa Fe!' For it is by this wholesale abbreviation that *La Villa Real de la Santa Fé de San Francisco de Asis* appears locally to be known.

I was most devastated to spot, far up a rock-strewn expanse, a most modest and unimpressive jumble of low adobe structures that barely stood up against the horizon. If he had told me instead, 'Look, Fray Alonso, at that tiny, ridiculous rock pile!' I would have been no more surprised.

Because of the lateness of the hour, we have camped some distance from the settlement. But my heart is in my feet. It is exactly as I had imagined. One hundred years ago, yes, it was plausible to send the estimable Coronado on his heroic journey this way to find the golden cities. But no golden cities have been found. Nor, it appears, will I find one. Surely Fray Luis, if he could see me now, would chuckle. Another rival wasting his career in the dreariest of provincial backwaters. At least a 'wild goose chase' would have had its moments of amusement.

Yet I pray You strengthen me not to grumble. Nor, for that matter, to prejudge the situation. This Santa Fe may be poor in size and grandeur, but still rich in heresy.

4 October

La Villa Real de la Santa Fé de San Francisco de Asis, capital of the New Mexico colony, home to a thousand or more natives and a hundred or more white men, emblem not of discovery but of all that was not found. The Seven Cities of Cibola – the very idea seems to mock this settlement. Yet still one hears talk of those cities – in the markets and already among my porters. People have not given up hope. How interesting. How pathetic, really. And distressing, the enduring power of this worldly myth.

We were taken at once to the parish church, on the eastern flank of the modest plaza. I was introduced to Fray Gonzago de Castelmonte de Santiago, the *custos*, another Franciscan. We Franciscans have had a virtual monopoly here, as the very name of the settlement would imply. Fray Gonzago has none of the suspicion or antipathy towards my mission that Fray Donaldo in Nuevo Leon was quick to demonstrate. But he was puzzled. Heresy, apostasy, backsliding, pagan and witch doctor rituals – these are matters of his daily concern insofar as they afflict his native flock, but he has seen no signs, he averred, none, of so-called European 'agitators'. Most tactfully, he recalled the previous special missions that the Holy Office sent here, which came before his time but which he understood to have borne little fruit. Nowadays, he concluded, it was simply a matter of treating the natives with patience, firmness, vigilant charity and occasional exemplary discipline. He predicted that in two generations to come, their loyalty to the Church and to His Hispanic Majesty as well, would be unswerving.

I reassured him that my arrival signaled no change in the Office's policy, which forbids the investigation of natives. And I made, once again, such apologies as I might for my own assignment.

But I did feel it appropriate, I said, that I review with him the common evidences of judaizing, only in the event he should observe them, or perhaps may already have unwittingly observed them in some European or other, or perhaps in natives who have been in contact with Europeans.

Among these, I mentioned to him the changing of linen for Saturday, the putting on of clean or festive clothes on Saturdays, a shyness with regard to the eating of pork, rabbit, or scaleless fish, calling children by Old Testament names, observing unusual fasts, reciting the Psalms without adding the *Gloria Patri* immediately after, washing corpses with warm water, lighting candles on Friday evenings earlier than on other evenings of the week, and, of course, circumcision.

Indeed, I may have enumerated virtually all of the accepted thirty-seven signs of the judaizer.

Fray Gonzago averred that he had neither seen nor heard of any such practices among his flock. Nonetheless, out of a spirit of generosity and openhandedness which confirmed my initial impression of Fray Gonzago, he offered that I test his conclusions by issuing an Edict of Faith. He would be happy to publicize it if I could remain the length of time necessary for his rather far-flung constituents, if they had evidence against any man or woman, to make the journey to Santa Fe to testify to that effect and present evidence.

I declared this to be an excellent plan, if one that necessitated a stay here – this I did not say aloud – longer than I had anticipated.

We concluded our meeting with a large meal of venison, haunch of bison and wine of Catalonia, that, notwithstanding the fact that it may have been in the barrel rather too long, was most welcome.

The drought we first encountered on the *altiplano* extends even to here. Apparently it is causing the game to become scarcer and begins to make the hunting tribes, particularly the so-called *Apache,* restless and a bit desperate. I count ourselves blessed that we encountered none of this on our journey.

5 October

Fray Gonzago has acted on our discussions with admirable efficiency. Today notices went out by horse that will soon reach every *hacienda* and *pueblo* within many leagues, indicating my presence here and the requirement that those with evidence of a full list of suspect practices on the part of any persons bring their testimony to me by the first of November.

Another excellent dinner this noontime, of pheasant and other victuals, including an altogether interesting concoction made with native corn that had been roasted. It is heartwarming to see our Spanish men being so adaptive to their new environment. Nonetheless, if I must wait here until November to take testimony, I am afraid I shall grow quite fat.

13 October

Something of an organizational crisis beset me today. Five of the men who came with me from Mexico, two muleteers, two porters and the cook, have declared their intention not to return. Apparently they got wind of some half-witted expedition that is being formulated to once more search for the Seven Cities. I pleaded and argued with them, that if Coronado could not find them, nor all the others in Coronado's wake, then what chance had they, after a hundred years had passed? Moreover that everyone of sound judgment now concurs that these were imaginative figments, in which men's greed reinterpreted the poor, spare *pueblos* as 'cities of gold'. It is easy to imagine how effective were my arguments, howsoever soundly reasoned. One does not easily argue with the lust for riches, especially when that lust has been stoked by legend. I do not fault men for dreaming, but I do fault them for sinful stupidity.

Nonetheless, their defection has left a large hole in my expedition. Fortunately I have time to fill it. I shall take care to take on only men with proven skill in firearms, so as to provide adequate deterrence in the event these *Apaches* dare to harass us.

17 October

I offer a prayer of thanks, for I have not only filled the vacancies in my expedition, but perhaps improved its overall functioning. All the new hires are excellent marksmen, except one who appears to possess no skill with arms whatsoever, but who, I decided, more than compensates for this deficiency by being a most excellent cook. Marksmanship is not his only deficiency. The man lacks the faculty of speech. He is mute. His hearing is unimpaired, and he does not appear stupid, he can nod yes or no to any question put to him. But some injury to his vocal chords, or perhaps some deserved punishment of Yours, has deprived him of words.

I believe I can live with this, given his culinary skills. And there is anyway far more talk on our journey, typically of the basest nature, than our spiritual purpose should have to countenance. I made him cook me a meal last night, before I offered him the job. I provided him with only such meager ingredients as we were likely to have deep into our journey: maize, potato, salt beef, a bit of sugar, and the like. To these, with my permission, he added certain native herbs and spices previously unknown to me, and the result was a stew as delicious as any I've partaken of since my departure from home. My stomach, I confess, is a bit of a tyrant. It demands I sacrifice one rifle in favor of its satisfaction. And at risk of the sin of gluttony, I concur.

7 November

It is now thirty-two days since notices were sent announcing my Edict of Faith, and not one man nor woman, native nor European, has appeared before me. I shall wait until the fifteenth, a date agreed between myself and Fray Gonzago as one that beyond any doubt would give witnesses every opportunity to appear.

And, of course, if there are no witnesses, and no suspects, there can be no *rich* suspects. I mention this only on account of my lingering suspicion that what Fray Luis attempted to turn the Inquisitor General's ear with when he proposed this wasted journey was the thought of confiscations. Fray Luis, reveling in his dreams of riches as absurd as the dreams of my lost muleteers! Or rather, tempting the Inquisitor General with such dreams. I declare it to be the gravest defect of our sacred organization that we are permitted to keep such wealth as comes our way as a result of convictions. It is the worst invitation to corruption. Dear God, I pray You grant me some sign whether my reasoning concerning this be true. I feel I myself am corruption's unintended (or perhaps not so unintended) victim at just this instant.

Oh, but the comeuppance Fray Luis may have, when I point out not only the lack of heretics in this barren region, but its poverty!

21 November

We have departed.

The initial stages of our return find us moving more rapidly than on our outbound journey. I attribute this either to the excellence of my new hires, which is what I would like to believe, or – which is far more likely – to the fact we are traveling downhill.

The new cook was superb last night. Alberto slew an antelope and I was delighted by the resulting ragout. So, I might add, was the entire expedition. Excellent for morale.

22 November

We have rejoined the Rio del Norte, which is already losing its mountain freshness in favor of the endless muddy meandering that even the fish must deplore.

We have seen nothing of the *Apache* raiding parties so much fretted about in Santa Fe. I begin to hope that Your blessing is upon our safe passage. I take care always to mention these *Apaches* in my prayers, as well as disease, drought, hunger, inclement weather and getting lost. I confess that in my arrogance I make a mental list, and endeavor to leave no hazard out.

26 November

A most extraordinary occurrence. I cannot yet tell whether it is fortune or misfortune, blessing or disaster.

Our cook, whom I have previously mentioned, and who the other men entitle 'the Dumb One' on account of his absence of conversation, has fallen under sharpest suspicion of the very crime that I was sent out to uncover and have hitherto nowhere found.

It came about as follows: we broke our march one half hour before sunset, as usual. It is my policy, now that the days are cooler, to give ourselves a bit more time before the onset of night to prepare camp. As is my wont, I wandered over to the area behind the mules where this so-called Dumb One had prepared his fire. He was busy with preparations, husking maize and the like, and could hardly have noticed my stunned gaze when I observed a candle lit a few feet from the fire, near where the food he had unpacked for the evening's meal was collected. There was nothing special about the candle, it was but one of the candles we customarily use, nor did the Dumb One make the smallest effort to conceal it. He didn't seem to think there was anything wrong in lighting a candle when darkness had not yet settled and when there was not another candle lit in the camp. Nor was the candle placed such as to be of any use in illuminating anything or in aiding him with his labors.

I thought at first it must be a candle he had used in lighting the cook fire. I indeed said to him, in an easy enough manner, 'So. Is that how you start your fire, by first lighting a candle?'

He didn't appear to know what I was talking about. He gave me that vacant look that well suits his face. He has eyes set far apart, an unappreciable nose, a thin mouth suited to silence and a shock of hair the color of sand that covers the majority of his brow. He has, in short, the look of some harlequin player, less the extravagant costume, of course. He is dressed in little better than rags, a small, youthful man. I repeated myself, I said to him, 'You used your candle to light the cook fire?'

He shook his head.

'No?' I asked. 'Then why do you light it? It is not yet dark.'

He lifted the candle questioningly.

'Yes. The candle. I understand why you light the cook fire.'

He hunched his shoulders, in protested ignorance.

By now I was already beginning to sense the facility of his pantomimes, as if these handful of gestures, which I could see might be repeated endlessly in minute variation, were his entire vocabulary, which he had crafted to meet his necessities.

'You must have a reason. People don't light candles for no reason,' I said.

His wide-set eyes beseeched me. I took this to mean that he was holding to whatever his shrug had meant.

'I don't follow,' I said. 'It is Friday evening, did you know that?'

He nodded.

'Do you always light such a candle on Friday evenings?'

He nodded again.

'Is it some sort of tradition with you?'

The same.

'Is it something from your family? Your mother?'

Yes, yes.

I do not believe I have previously encountered anyone who in such circumstances acted as if he had less to hide. Was he guileless? Was he fearless?

'But did your mother have a reason to light a candle?' I asked.

His eyes now narrowed, perhaps wondering why I was asking such odd questions.

'Your mother. Her *reason*.' I perhaps made silly gesticulations myself, as if his were a pidgin tongue I was attempting to emulate.

Now he made a kind of upward spiral with his finger, a gesture, I supposed, of ongoingness.

'Her reason was the same as yours? It was *her* tradition?'

He smiled broadly in agreement, pleased that we were now in easy communication.

I decided I must lay out a few markers for him, to be sure I was being understood. 'The issue, sir, is not simply whether you light a candle, but whether you light one particularly on Friday nights, and not for illumination or some other practical purpose, but precisely for the reason you seem to ascribe, namely, tradition. You do it to remember your mother, she to remember hers, and so on back through history, all of it prescribed by law, of which you may be only dimly aware, but which lives through the very tradition to which you admit. Am I far off here?'

The Dumb One smiled broadly at me. At that moment I imagined he might be simple as well as mute. In truth, I was stunned by his good nature. I decided to ask no more questions. Doubtless this was my prosecutorial experience at work, knowing to quit when one has reached the point of maximum advantage. The Dumb One returned to his labors and produced a most excellent dinner of cod and maize. With every morsel of food I ate, I wondered, and prayed for guidance.

Dear God, by Your grace and pity which open the path of salvation even to those who murdered Your only begotten Son, I see that the evidence of judaizing is overwhelming. But what action shall I take?

THE DUMB ONE

Entries from 27 November to 25 December 1649

I have placed the Dumb One under a form of arrest.

During night while we sleep he shall be bound and tied to a tree, lest he escape in the darkness.

During the day he will march with the rest of us; however if he attempts to escape, the others are ordered, if no other means of apprehension succeeds, to shoot him.

I explained all this to the Dumb One. He accepted it with what I can only describe as an equanimity of spirit. A furrowed brow and his hands raised emptily were the only indications by which I could discern that he wished to know the reasons for my actions. I explained to him that I was an emissary of the Holy Office and that he was under suspicion of heresy.

Then a puzzled look, at the very end of my explanation, as if the word 'heresy' meant nothing to him.

'What is "heresy"? You don't know even that much?' From his

continuing puzzlement it appeared not, so I continued: 'Heresy is when a Christian holds beliefs that are at odds with Christian teaching.'

It seemed as if each word that I pronounced, 'heresy,' 'Christian', 'beliefs', 'odds', 'teaching', were proceeding through his brain, each after the other, for inspection, consideration. His lips quivered, giving a fleeting impression of movement, with, of course, no words coming forth.

But was he understanding what I said?

His gaze had an astonishing steadiness to it. I could not be sure if, in his own quiet, inexpressive way, he was not mocking me. Yet there was no curl to his lip, no glint to his eye. He appeared to try to pronounce my last words. His lips did indeed move, however with such slurred motion that it was apparent he had never used them for actual speech.

'What is "Christian teaching"? Is that what you are asking?'

He nodded with childish enthusiasm.

'Christian teaching,' I said, 'is the truth of our religion, passed from one generation to the next.'

I confess that my explanation was a meager one. Yet I was hardly prepared for the depth of his puzzlement. I was beginning to dread the deep furrows of his brow, which appeared all the more profound for perturbing so innocent and unlined a face.

Dear Lord and Savior, what an impatient communicator of Your word I am.

'What? What are you asking? What a "generation" is?' I asked.

He shook his head no.

'Then what? What do you not grasp? "The truth of our religion"?'

His expression at once changed to delight.

'Do you know nothing?' I said with annoyance.

If my aim was to ignite in him some greater response by means of humiliation, I failed. He took no offence. He made no effort to answer my accusation. He simply laid eyes on me. I could begin to see how his very disability might become his weapon, his best defense.

I resolved then, rather than to ply him with the a-b-c's of Christian truth, of which surely he had to be aware no matter how benighted his upbringing, to be careful with this Dumb One. There is something naïve about him, and yet... what?

The fact is, I *must* be careful with him. He is all I have to show for my labors, the only game in my bag.

I determined further that the Dumb One must not continue to be our cook. He seems even-tempered and accepting, but how can I be sure that faced with my declared suspicions of him, he would not resort to some awful means against us, which only a cook would have the chance to succeed at? He could kill us all!

It is not enough that he does not seem the type. Is it not the essence of the *Marrano* to deceive, to keep a deep secret alive?

I have asked Arroyo Ricardo to take on the added responsibility of cooking. At least he knows how to build a reliable fire. My stomach shall bear the brunt of this sacrifice.

Meanwhile I search Your Holy Scripture to learn if muteness is a sign of the Devil.

28 November

Last evening we were served the most execrable meal I have perhaps eaten in my life. The beans tasted like stones washed in sewer water.

Despite the difficulties that his speechlessness presents, I have determined to attempt a proper interrogation of the Dumb One. Perhaps, after all, I was wildly overhasty in my surmises. Hunger for a success of any kind, not to say boredom, can do that to a man.

I shall question him tomorrow, after the day's journey.

29 November

I will record as much of my interrogation of the Dumb One as I can faithfully recall.

I approached him after the evening meal in that place to which the porters had consigned him for the night. In furtherance of my instructions, they had attached him by rope to the sturdiest tree the campsite afforded.

For purposes of our talk, I loosened his bonds, which in any case were far from tight. (I have instructed one and all of our men that suspicion is not conviction, and no means shall be applied to this man, by intention or guilty negligence, that could be considered punishment of any sort.)

He was not displeased to see me. He bore me no evident

grudge for his confinement and demotion, and even seemed eager for the opportunity to spend time with me, man to man, so to speak.

We sat on the blanket which he had been given, I with my legs outstretched and he with legs folded at the knee one under the other, in the Indian fashion. I began with what I supposed was the most basic question of all, 'Do you believe in the Holy Trinity, of the Father, the Son and the Holy Spirit?'

I shall remember his extraordinary answer – if it was an answer at all – until the end of my days. He shrugged.

No 'yes', no 'no', no nods nor shakes of the head, nothing clearly one way or the other. Only a shrug.

'Do you believe that Mary the Mother of God gave birth to Jesus Christ Our Lord and Savior while a virgin?' I asked.

Again, his dreadful, uncommitted shrug.

'Do you believe in the bodily resurrection of Jesus Christ Our Lord and Savior?' I asked.

For a third time, his shrug.

Though at this junction, I must say, he looked entirely sad. A sadness, if I could further characterize it, pure unto itself, untainted with guilt or rue.

'You have answered none of my questions yea or nay,' I said. 'Do your shrugs imply that in fact you do not believe in the Trinity, the Virgin Birth and the Resurrection? For belief requires affirmation. Doubt is closer kin to unbelief.'

Then his sadness seemed to deepen, until it seemed to weigh on him like a stone.

'It would be a happy thing, for your salvation, if your heart could answer yea,' I said.

He nodded heavily.

'Then why can it not?'

He continued to nod, as if by some compulsion, since a nod, as far as I could discern, made no sense at all as an answer to my question.

Nodding at what? Nodding why?

I became aware that I might be utterly misinterpreting every sign this Dumb One made. How could I know what he meant? I was living in a universe of my own surmises.

I cut the interrogation short. I said to the Dumb One that I would like to resume our talk soon. He nodded, and the slightest smile curled his lip. Was he telling me that he would like that?

30 November

I record that on this day, the thirtieth of November, we regained the Rio Bravo. Thus we are ahead of schedule.

1 December

Tonight I put to the Dumb One all the recognized signs of judaizing. With vigorous, unmistakable head shakes, he denied all of them, except the lighting of a candle on Friday evening. He was even eager, and for a moment I feared he might be overeager, to show me the proof that he was not circumcised. Though first he made me explain to him what circumcision was. I still am not certain that when he displays such incomprehension he is not feigning something. But, in truth, the more often it happens, the more I am inclined to think he is simply ignorant.

An odd mix he is, of a certain kind of awareness on the one hand, and ignorance of almost the entire world on the other. It must come, I suppose, from a life lived in the wasteland of these northern deserts. His cooking, for instance, he appears to have learned not only from his mother but from familiarities with natives.

For the record: the Dumb One is indeed uncircumcised.

5 December

Tonight I went back on my pledge not to question the Dumb One further about matters to which his answers must remain suspect and unclear. I asked him to state clearly, by one head gesture or the other, whether he believed that our Lord Jesus Christ died for our sins. My eminently reasonable and simply-put question was greeted, once more, with a version of his shrug which struck me this time as so impertinent, arrogant, impious and craven that I began to shake the Dumb One with righteous vigor, hoping to shake some sense into him at last. I utterly failed in this. He simply regarded me with the hurt eyes of a beaten cur. But my fervor may have had an unexpected benefit. It loosened from underneath the Dumb One's tunic a small leather pouch, which he wore around his neck. I had never seen this before.

I asked him what it contained.

He made that spiraling gesture with his finger that I had come to understand meant his ancestors, or his mother in particular.

'It came from your mother?'

He nodded that it did. 'But what is it?' I asked again.

He shrugged.

'Is it a jewel perhaps? Because if it is a jewel, it rather calls attention to itself, hung by your neck like that, you might wish to take greater precautions –'

He shook his head vigorously. It was not a jewel.

'Oh. What is it, then? A stone?'

No.

'A tooth?'

No.

'A piece of paper?'

The Dumb One nodded decisively.

'So it's a bit of paper which your mother gave you, and told you to hold dear in this pouch?'

Again, his decisive nod.

'What sort of paper, then, that your mother told you to hold dear? Of course, forgive me, you can't answer that. But is it in a strange writing?'

He nodded that it was.

'May I see it, perhaps? Perhaps I can read it to you, so you will know what it says.'

The Dumb One backed slightly away from me and put the pouch back into his tunic where it could not be seen.

'Did your mother tell you to hold it safe from the eyes of others?'

He nodded yes.

'But are we not friends? Perhaps I can help you.'

He shook his head no.

And there I let it rest. My only recourse that I could see at that moment was to strip the pouch from him by force, and then I would surely have had an alien and sullen being on my hands. I must exercise caution. I must recognize my limitations. We are hundreds of leagues from anywhere.

Nonetheless, the presence of that pouch around his neck, and the way he holds it dear, and his confirmation of my query concerning the writing's strangeness, all these add inevitably to my suspicion.

And if the writing is in Hebrew?

9 December

A day of calamity, a day of infamy! Today a raiding party of *Apaches* attacked us in the late morning hours. They appeared out of the southeast, numbering twenty or twenty-five savages, their faces painted and feathered and their horses robed, frightful in appearance, with bows and arrows, and at least one carried a musket, acquired doubtless in some previous bloody event. Never had I seen the very image of a Satanic cult so entirely personified.

And yet at first we hoped their intentions might be peaceful, or at worst we might ward them off with one supply or another, spirits or salt beef or even one of our mules. They approached us from the eastern bank of the river, fording it with some delicacy and patience, arms upraised as if in peace.

At my order we did likewise with our arms, hoping our mimicking of their behavior would confirm our openness and candor. At the same time, each of our armed muleteers drew instinctively close to his weapons. There was never a chance to flee, not with these *Apaches* on horseback and we with our mules alone. All civilized men must rue the day the savages stole their first horse.

Their attack came immediately and without a warning as they emerged from the muddy bath of the river. No sooner had we stopped our progress and turned to them with goodwill and calculated hopes than they drew their assorted weapons and made their charge. Before we fired a shot, two of our own, Lucio and the most able Alberto, fell with mortal wounds from tomahawk or arrow.

The savages raced up and down our ranks, running through then turning and running through again. I prayed for our wretched lives. The *Apaches* grasped at our mules and saddlebags, in many instances snatching them away. Two more men fell.

It was only with the first round of our weapon-fire that the tide of battle, so to speak, in any way altered. We unhorsed one *Apache* and they kept a distance and did not at once charge us again. We rained as much fire on them as the fewness of our arms, compared to their numbers, allowed.

And I was most astonished to see, and indeed most gratified, that the very Dumb One whom I had arrested and suffered to endure such numerous interrogations, picked up the weapons of the fallen Alberto and acquitted himself with valor. Far from hiding himself close to the ground or among the mules so as to minimize his exposure, he ran after these *Apaches* a considerable distance, shaking an enraged fist and firing one-handedly.

I imagine it was only with Your grace that he was not shot from behind by one of our own, so far out front was he.

Withal, the Dumb One's heroics and our steady fire, the savages decided they had had enough of us and retreated across the river with one of our mules. They seemed well-satisfied with their treasure, though in exchange for it they had left one of their own on the ground and their booty was no more than they might have had without a shot fired. That they will shed such blood and spread such mayhem for a few days' provisions is perhaps the fiercest indictment of their barbarism.

We mounted our own dead on our remaining animals and

continued our march as rapidly as circumstances allowed. Tonight we all, to a man, dug graves for Lucio and our cherished huntsman Alberto, who died before having even a chance to show their Christian valor. These graves are a little up the bank from the Rio Bravo. It is possible that flood conditions will one day wash them away, but we are not in circumstances where we can reconnoiter too widely for a more appropriate site.

The *Apaches*, I presume, will come back for their own dead. They are said not to be too primitive for that, but for myself I would put no inhumanity past them.

The attack and resulting losses have shaken our entire expedition. On completion of the grave-digging, I called for a special service of prayer. Even the Dumb One, I observed, bowed his head and prayed with vigor, tears in his eyes, as there were in the eyes of some others.

Dear Jesus my Savior, I pray Your forgiveness for the casual and even jaunty tone I struck elsewhere in this journal about welcoming the distraction of Indian attacks. They are not amusements.

Today has also caused me to reevaluate my prisoner. When circumstances were gone awry, when he had the easy chance to take up a weapon and escape, he did not. On the contrary, he used that weapon to our great advantage, and made an example for the others.

I thanked him, in simple words, for his contribution.

12 December

A heaviness, and a wariness, continue to hover over our expedition as a result of the recent attack. I am sleeping poorly, and not only on account of the snakes.

The temperatures now drop toward freezing at night. Our blankets are thin and barely sufficient, but shall have to do. I have considered giving the Dumb One his freedom after dark, and furthermore, the thought of restoring him to his post as cook has crossed my mind, or I should say, my stomach. But his odd self-confidence, his absence of fear, even his naïve trustfulness, still unnerve me. Where do they come from, I wonder each time I observe them. Dear God, forgive me my excess of caution, if such it be. I am too fearful of making mistakes. And yet this Dumb One, I am certain, looms large as one of those mistakes that I might make.

13 December

Today we marched all day through muddy flats in heavy rain. The wet season has apparently arrived, with its attendant delays and inconveniences.

18 December

Our misfortunes multiply.

Yesterday, two of the men, Hector and our scout Arroyo Ricardo, fell ill with fevers and vomiting. So severe was their indisposition that they became unable to travel and we halted for the day.

19 December

Today three more men took ill. All now vomit blood. It is truly some plague that is upon us. At every hour we pray for relief.

We remain at the same muddy outpost of the river where we halted our march yesterday, two hundred leagues yet from Monterrey.

Our medicines are few and without effect. We use the river water to make cold compresses. Nothing helps. Five men in agony, and myself as well on account of their sufferings. Arroyo Ricardo has a family, wife and sons, and wailed today in fear of never seeing their faces again.

Dear Lord who hears our prayers, I make no appeal to Your justice, but only Your mercy. May Your wretched servants not perish in this awful wilderness, may Arroyo Ricardo be granted the loving visages of his family once again.

20 December

Their last rites having been given, Hector, Miguel and Tomas all died in the night. I have ordered their bodies burned out of hygienic necessity and our camp to move at least a modest distance downriver. I myself feel the onset of fever, though I resist it. Two more of the men fell ill during the same hours when death took the three. Now our entire expedition save five are afflicted.

I myself have just begun to vomit.

Shall none of us feel civilization's embraces ever again? I have observed even the Dumb One seeming to say his prayers.

21 December

I detail the symptoms of this plague: fever, vomiting, blood, uncontrolled stool, rashes in some cases but not all.

Arroyo Ricardo died before dawn. Last rites administered. I additionally shed a tear: his great fear came to pass. Who among us will live to tell Arroyo Ricardo's family that he died thinking of them?

The Dumb One has come to me with a request that he be allowed to go beyond our sight in search of native herbs and medicines that might help us. I am weakened myself, but questioned him sufficiently to determine that this is a subject he may know something about. I sent him off with one of the few others among us still healthy, Felipe, as his helper and, yes, minder.

21 December

later

In the last hours I have grown pitifully weak and now for the first time have vomited blood. What will become of us? Will this journal be all that remains someday to tell the tale? I fear I am growing too weak to write.

You by whose infinite mercy and grace may the shadow of doubt never cross my heart: I pray do not forsake us.

22 December

All ill save the Dumb One, Felipe and Ramon.

Three more deaths. Last rites, bodies burnt, awful odors in the smoke.

I cannot stand, I cannot do aught.

I am in a dream.

25 December

I record the following as hallucination, or miracle, or manifestation of malign interest.

It appears that continuously, during my unwakingness and ever since returning from his desert hunts, the Dumb One has been brewing teas and soups with the herbs and stuffs that he acquired there, and has been feeding them to us all, the healthy and sick, the awake and hallucinatory. Two men, already gravely suffering, died after having imbibed these potions, but the rest remained well or, in my case, last night, on the eve of our Savior's birthday, commenced to recover. This Dumb One, indeed, as the instrument of Your divine purpose, may have facilitated the saving of my life.

I was meditating on this remarkable fact last evening, as he hovered over me administering the herbs he had gathered. My mind cleared as if a smoky fire had been put out. Confusion lingered but I knew I was alive. Whilst I lay and watched with half-shut eyes his modest movements of care, placing certain patches in hot water, others in cold, applying them to my neck and my feet, I came to consider the sum of good deeds that I could now attribute to this Dumb One. And upon doing so, I was struck with the keenest sadness. For it became immediately apparent to me that no matter the sum of his charities and kindnesses, none of them could earn him even one instant of salvation, since they were not performed in the name of You our Lord and Savior. My sorrow, of course, was for his damnation. But it was soon accompanied by scorn for my own pride, that I should imagine for an instant second-guessing the infinite wisdom of Your grace, which beyond men's understanding chooses who shall see the truth and who shall not. And both my sorrow and scorn then gave way, I confess, to rage. Yes, rage, even in my fever and weakness, at this Dumb One himself, for not rushing at every instant and with every fiber of his being to seek You out. How could he be so good and such a fool at once? It was then, as I castigated him with my concentrated mind and composed dire warnings to deliver that his goodnesses would be of no help whatsoever in the heavenly scales of judgment if they were not done through Your embrace, that I heard a voice, the Dumb One's voice, as I then surmised. The voice said, 'I live as if there is a God.'

I was struck, I do confess, not so much at first by the outrage of these blasphemous words as by the manifestation of this voice itself.

For I 'heard' it and yet I did not hear it. I attributed it to the Dumb One because he was ministering to me at the time and because I could dimly sense how it could be thought a kind of answer to my meditations. Yet I shall have difficulty further describing this voice. It had no tone that I could describe, nor even words. The words I attribute to it are rather like my pure understanding of them, my translation, as it were. It was as if a being were close to me, whispering pure thought, in a whisper that was not a whisper.

Now, this evening, I am stronger. I am no longer in a dream-like state. It is a miracle, without a doubt, for which I give continuous thanks. Of all our expedition, only Felipe, Ramon, the Dumb One and I remain alive. But as grateful as I am for life and breath, dear Lord, I am troubled by this 'voice'. No, more than troubled, deeply vexed. I went to the Dumb One. I said to him, 'While you minded me, while I was in a "state", did you think to say to me, did you have the thought, or did even your expression mean to convey the thought, "I live as if there is a God"?'

In that childish way of his, he nodded enthusiastically that he had. If it had been only his nod, I would have been less troubled, but even as he nodded, I heard the selfsame 'voice' again, saying 'A God of love'.

For a moment I became exasperated, fearing he was playing some game with me, like some jester who has learned to throw his voice. 'Did you just say something again?' I demanded.

But he only shrugged. And I heard no 'voice'.

Let me confess further the depth of my confusion. My faith in You proceeds, by Your grace, through a sense of closeness, of intimacy. Behind the veils of shape and color and time, I sense Your ineffable presence in all that is. I look at my hand, I see Your hand. I hear a chime, I hear Your harmony and song. In the interconnection of all things, in the flux of the world, just out of sight and hearing, I sense Your order. In the rough-and-tumble of our human feelings, I intimate Your mercy. In the edifice of Your Holy Church, I know Your truth. Yet this 'voice', which I feel certain came from the Dumb One, in my well and waking state no less than in my ill and dreamy one, had in its seeming formation the same closeness, even perhaps the same intimation of love, that certifies my unshakable faith in You. Indeed, were it not for my faith, I might conclude that my own mind in some incomprehensible perturbation had manufactured it. I pray for a sign: Heavenly Father, what has truly happened on this day of Your Son's birth? Surely it is Your work? Surely it is not Satan's? But then what am I to make of my judaizing heretic?

THE VOICE

Entries from 26 December 1649 to 10 January 1650

Tonight I asked such questions of the Dumb One as my strength permitted. I consumed a bit of soup this evening. He continues to attend to me.

My questions, I must admit, were designed to elicit what I have called his 'voice'. I asked him all manner of things, about his background, his education, if any, his experience of the world, the customs of his people – and here, of course, I would not have been entirely surprised to find judaizing habits.

It seemed at first that the 'voice' must have been a figment of my overheated constitution, which now, as my fever has departed, should not return. Our dialogue was as on previous occasions, before the plague struck. I asked questions. He nodded or shook his head in denial and I could conclude but little, since my questions were not chiefly of a yes-or-no nature, but instead asked for broader discussions.

For the record, he denied coming from Santa Fe, he denied having a Jewess or *Marrano* for mother, he denied knowing what I meant by *Marrano,* and he denied a knowledge of witchcraft, the Talmud, or the Portuguese language.

Throughout my questioning, he busied himself preparing a tea. When it was properly steeped, he poured me a cup of it. The tea had a peculiar and bitter aftertaste. Medicinal, I supposed. I sipped it rather determinedly, not wishing to insult its maker nor miss out on some fortifying value which his other preparations had possessed, though I could not help imagining that this one had been concocted from straw. The Dumb One was working his fire, paying me seeming little mind, when I again heard the 'voice'. 'My father's father's father rode with Coronado,' it 'said' directly to my mind.

When my surprise subsided, I could scarcely hold back an unworthy amusement. 'Did you just now intend to convey to me something about your father's father's father?' I asked him.

He looked up from the cook fire with an expression of puzzlement. 'Did your father's father's father ride with Coronado?' I asked.

He assented with a broad grin.

'You have conquistador blood in you?'

I confess that a trace of mockery, even hilarity, without a doubt seeped into my voice then.

He again grinned toothily.

The 'voice' resumed. 'I come from near El Paso del Norte,' it said. 'My father traveled. He brought goods to the *pueblos* and *haciendas.* I don't know if native blood was in my parents' veins. But the blood of Don Tomas Rodrigues de Santangel was for sure.'

'A conquistador?' I said again. 'Don Tomas Rodrigues de Santangel?' In truth, I am not sure if I said this aloud, or only in my mind's precincts, in answer to the voice. In either event, I was mystified. This Dumb One, this illiterate son of a frontier peddler, descended from a conquistador? Though of course one could not help but think of the numbers of Spaniards of that era who left behind more than memories with the native women.

The voice continued. 'This is what my father said. My mother's people I never knew. They came from the south. She missed them very much. My mother was a pious woman. She took me to church.'

'And lit Friday candles to remember her mother!' I most certainly said this much aloud.

The Dumb One nodded enthusiastically, though whether in response to my words alone or because he had created or heard the 'voice' that preceded them I could not say with certainty.

27 December

A very nearly sleepless night. Fears, questions, prayers. Was the 'voice' of the Dumb One a miracle, or a snare of illusion? What use was it, what truth was in it? You or Satan? Satan or You?

This morning I appear to have received an answer to my incessant prayers. It came to me, as such answers often do, as I performed my ablutions.

Dear God, have I heard You rightly when I declare that this 'voice' of the Dumb One is Your means of aiding me in my investigation of this mute creature, and thus of facilitating the possibility that I might help to save him?

It is so! It must be so! Every fiber of my mind and heart tell me that it is so! For Satan obfuscates, Satan obscures, whereas this 'voice' tells me what I need to know about the fallen creature in my care.

Praise be the Lord who makes and dissolves mysteries, who brings light to darkness, who provides all that is necessary and proper for man to find his way to Him!

28 December

We regroup. We move on. What choice is there? It is both a necessity and our obligation, to say the least.

I am able to walk a bit and to ride a bit. Today I ate hard food, a bit of salt beef, for the first time. It tasted to my tongue like desiccated leather.

Our catastrophic losses force a change in our organization. We have lost a scout, but I shall not replace him one-for-one. We will simply retrace the river routes that brought us from Monterrey. I should think that would be feasible, even with my poor memory for direction. Since neither our mules nor our supplies suffered, it is possible for us now to jettison some items in favor of freeing one mule to carry two of us at once. We are terribly behind our imagined schedule, but perhaps by this means some time can be recaptured. And my still-fragile health succored.

The situation of the Dumb One requires deeper consideration. I have thanked him amply and repeatedly for both the help he provided and his stalwart manner in providing it. I am hugely impressed by his loyalty, one of the most admirable virtues. But there is more to it than gratitude for his actions. I have come to appreciate even how he walks, without gravity or great intention, but rather with an easy, light step, as if he were a visitor in this world. He does not anger easily, or perhaps at all. In truth, I have never seen him angry. He appears to accept what is done to him, and how others are. One might accuse him of passivity, but his contributions at moments of danger belie it. Despite the fallen and damned state in which I find him, I remain convinced in some remote corner of my being that salvation is not beyond him. I tell myself that he may have simply been the victim of unfortunate circumstances and influences.

Yet if he should run away from us, not only would we who remain suffer grievously on account of his loss, but I would surely be held accountable on my return. I can almost hear the word 'negligence', or even 'recklessness', flowing from Fray Luis's honeyed lips. It is a pity to hold the Dumb One, and my own sense of Christian fairness and recompense, hostage to such considerations. And yet I cannot deny that I am part of a mission larger than myself.

What to decide?

I come down on the side of mercy and chance. I shall explain to the Dumb One the trust I am placing in him and how I will suffer badly if he disappoints me and runs away. At the same time I will no longer bind him and I will restore him to his place as our cook. I will even allow him candles.

29 December

The first result of my decision regarding the Dumb One is that we have once again, those of us who remain, enjoyed a meal of delicious food. Grilled and skewered meats, exquisitely spiced. I am regaining my full strength. I don't doubt that the excellent sustenance contributes to the rapidity of my progress.

As for the miracle of the Dumb One's voice, thanks to our Lord and Savior, I note the following:

One, it only presents itself to my mind when I am in the Dumb One's presence.

Two, it only presents itself in answer to questions I have put to him, aloud or otherwise.

Three, the Dumb One does not seem aware that his mind has 'spoken' to me, yet every significant fact the voice alleges, the Dumb One with his limited yet competent gestures is able to confirm.

I have not had communication with it since it informed me of the Dumb One's conquistador ancestor.

Though I should make one further notation regarding the 'voice'. I have attempted previously to describe how it appears to my mind. On re-reading the preceding entries, it occurs to me to specify that when I record the 'voice' in this journal, and in particular when I record thoughts of a more complicated or extended nature, I without a doubt add words, phrases, even sentences, that do not appear to my mind in such complete and coherent form. Rather, the 'voice' is all of a piece, a simultaneous, as it were, conveyance of insight; and it is only when I, so to speak, transcribe the voice, that all the words, like flakes of snow when they crystallize from raindrops, appear in their proper Spanish form.

30 December

Tonight, in the Dumb One's presence, and while we sat at the cook fire in quiet, my mind wordlessly asking him questions, the 'voice' returned and answered me.

I asked once again if he believed in our faith's eternal truths.

The voice answered, 'I can only believe what in my mind is true.'

'Oh, and how does your mind determine what is true?' I asked. 'Especially if you cannot read?'

'My mother could read,' the voice said. 'She read books to me.'

'And what books were those?' I wordlessly asked.

'The Bible,' the voice said. 'And books of wisdom.'

'Books of magic!'

'Not magic, sir. Wisdom,' the voice insisted.

'Names. Tell me names.'

'Souza, a very wise man,' the voice said.

'Souza? Who is Souza?'

'A very wise man of Holland,' the voice said.

'Oh, of Holland. Yes of course!'

I might have ceased my interrogation there. Everything had become clearer. The candles, the mother, the Sephardic-Jewish name 'Souza'!

Nonetheless I continued, conveying wordlessly to the voice, in what I thought a mild and inviting manner, 'If it is your mind you obey, does it not impress your mind that so many of the world's wisest and most learned men, St. Paul, St. Augustine, Thomas Aquinas, Ignatius Loyola, and so on, have agreed in holding our Church's doctrines to be true and correct? Do you not believe these were men more learned than yourself, all of whom came to the same conclusions?'

'This is authority you speak about. Not mind,' the Dumb One's voice replied.

'Why is that so?' I asked in silence. 'We all know of problems that tax the most diligent minds, and none more so than the great problems of our earthly existence. Is it not reasonable for a man to feel humble when confronting them, and to seek the counsel of those more wise and clever than himself?'

'I do not know these men you speak about. If they are wise, I will listen. But my mind must decide,' the voice said. 'Or else I am a slave.'

'And if your mind should be a faulty instrument, more so than the minds of these whom I assure you were wise beyond compare?'

'Then I am myself a faulty instrument,' the voice said. 'But I am still the instrument that I am.'

'And this instrument that is you, is it so faulty that it might not be persuaded by the evident fact that our Christian civilization, the civilization of those who believe in the Holy Trinity and the Virgin Birth and the Resurrection, has made achievements far superior to all others, in buildings and music and books and all the arts and sciences, all around the globe. Is it not now the case that Christianity is triumphant more than others? Does this not suggest the truth of our beliefs?'

'No, not truth. I don't think. I think it suggests power,' the voice said.

I fear I am not capturing the tone with which the voice wordlessly stated these matters. It was as if it delighted in having the opportunity, so to speak, to debate with me. Perhaps it was the Dumb One's arrogance (for I could not help but attribute any characteristic of the voice to the Dumb One himself). Or perhaps he was only grateful for having someone to speak to, regardless of the circumstances. What most shocked me, surely, was that such an illiterate, uneducated wretch of the desert could even entertain such sophisticated, if catastrophically misguided, thoughts. All I could do was to praise God, who puts surprises in the soul of every man!

I continued: 'And is your mind not impressed by the magnificent and well-attested miracles which confirm our faith, and which, such is their power, could only have been sanctioned by God?'

'It is impressed,' the voice said.

'Ah! So your mind does believe in such things! Its reason is not so crabbed and stunted a thing that it rules out what it cannot itself imagine!'

'But miracles are everywhere,' the voice said. 'Every religion has miracles. Who is to say which are the greatest and the most true? There are too many miracles! And one is in support of one truth, and another in support of another, and each religion denies the other religion the same as each miracle denies the other miracle. But if one miracle can be, then all can be! It makes me dizzy!'

It was at this shocking moment of confession that I stopped for the night. Throughout the period of our dialogue, the Dumb One had sat scrubbing his pots and utensils, as if oblivious to all that coursed through my mind. Yet when at the conclusion I asked him about each particular, he confirmed, to the extent his inarticulate gestures could, every one of them. He did so with the same fearless, matter-of-fact enthusiasm that his voice had evinced in my mind.

I discover one further argument why the 'voice' is not Satan's:

I am not in the slightest tempted to believe one word the Dumb One avows. I am simply the witness to his words. I am the doctor who must find his cure.

2 January 1650

Another 'discussion' with the Dumb One this evening.

This time I was lectured, of all things, about the comparative virtues of the different religions! Absolutely astounding! That he should have the casual audacity to lecture an official of the Holy Office on the virtues of the Moors. 'They are clean, honorable, poetic, sincere,' and, to boot, in measures perhaps greater than the Christian! And the Jew, with his sagacity and family piety and love of justice, again, in measures greater than the Christian. What has the Christian got, according to this wretched voice of the desert? Well, yes, he grants us the Christian virtues, he grants us charity and mercy and so on. But must we take a lesson even from the native tribes of America? These, he claims, are superior in their closeness to nature. 'But nature is fallen!' I demanded. 'Nature is their damnation!'

'This isn't proved,' said the Dumb One's voice.

I finally lost all sense of myself. 'Nothing is proved except your imbecility!' I shouted in my mind. 'If a little learning is dangerous, then a speck of learning can be only a catastrophe! Don't you see how you condemn yourself eternally?'

'Do I have the power?'

'Every man has the power! Has not God endowed man with free will? Did not your mother's tales of magic and insolence tell you even that much?'

As always, I attempted to confirm the voice's veracity through simple questionings of the Dumb One. I was astonished that when laid out for his yea-or-nay, he continued to deny nothing.

At one point I leaned forward and squeezed his upper arms severely, as if to squeeze sense into him, and yelled into his face, 'I wonder why I waste my time with you!'

He seemed puzzled by my outburst.

Dear God, who has provided this miracle of the Dumb One's voice so that his secret sins may see the light of correction, hear once again my thanks for Your help in my humble task.

4 January

Another futile discussion this evening. I say 'futile', but Holy Father I do not presume to chart the depths of Your meanings and ways. All I must confess is that there were moments tonight when I felt certain I should ring the heretic's neck then and there.

We sat, as usual, close to the fire, he and I alone.

There was a great deal of back-and-forth between the voice and myself this night, but I will record it all as best I can. I began by asking if he had ever seen a Jew.

'No,' the voice replied. 'Not in person. None that I know.'

'Or a Moor?'

'No.'

'So when the other night you described to me what a Moor was like and what a Jew was like, these descriptions were only from things your mother had read to you?'

'Yes.'

'But if you know so much about Jews, would it not stand to reason you would know that lighting a candle on Friday evenings is a Jewish practice?'

'I knew it was a Jewish practice,' the voice said. 'But that wasn't why I did it. Or my mother either. My mother was a good Christian.'

'I would be more inclined to believe what you say,' I said, 'except that you deny every article of our Christian faith. You have no faith. Are you sure you don't have Jewish faith?'

'I am sure,' the voice said.

'Do you believe that the Jews are a special people, chosen by God?'

'No.'

'Do you believe there is a Messiah yet to come?'

'No.'

'Are you aware that one of the most fundamental tenets of Jewish practice is the lighting of the sabbath candle?'

'I told you why I do it,' the voice said.

'But you could cease.'

'Why should I?'

'To prove to me at least that you are not a judaizer. Are you perhaps unaware, was it in none of your mother's books, the history that forged our Holy Office? The *reconquista* with its attendant popular excesses, the unification of Aragon and Castile, the ultimatums of our most wise Majesties Ferdinand and Isabella, all these put pressure on those Jews who during the dark epoch of Moorish rule had been allowed to thrive. Therefore throughout the fifteenth century, in large numbers they converted to Our Holy Faith, a glorious triumph, or so it seemed, until it was uncovered that many did so for the most base of motives, to save their necks or their property, while lacking inward belief. Many of these New Christians, these *conversos* or *Marranos*, indeed continued secretly to maintain their ancient Jewish practice, even while on Sundays they went to Church and on weekdays, due to the undeniable ambition and drive of the Jew, more and more made themselves indispensable to the State. You must try to imagine how both the kingdom and the Church came to danger. We were being eaten away from within, by the insincerity not of all but of enough. And this is why our Holy Office of the Inquisition was born, to oppose that danger and to root out that insincerity. And when the insincerity fled to the New World, the Holy Office followed it there, so that these vast lands we have acquired for Christian truth at the cost of Christian blood, shall not similarly be undermined and lost. Is all that clear?'

'It is clear,' the voice said. 'But it isn't possible to make a man believe something by force.'

'It isn't?'

'If there is force, then only the results of force can speak from a man, not the results of belief.'

'And how can you be so sure of this?' I asked.

'My mind tells me,' the voice said.

These words of the Dumb One's voice, so bleakly self-sufficient, so endlessly circular in their defense of the indefensible, caused me to think again of that pouch around his neck. Perhaps it is as he claims about the candle. Perhaps he does it as a habit of memory and love without connection to a Judaic intent. But his self-confessed heresies of every description, his utter inability to confess to faith of any kind, in yet so guileless a figure, leads me to look at the bulge beneath his neck – for his tunic again covers up the pouch – with very nearly a longing that it might contain some answer. That it might contain, actually, the proof of his Judaism that his mother has passed onto him.

Once again, the Dumb One cheerfully confirmed what his voice had told me in the privacy of my mind.

6 January

It is an interesting question, how to show Christian love on a daily basis to a man whom one is potentially taking to be burned. Of course I do not expect that latter result. I expect success in turning his course. I expect a reconciliation.

But is not my keeping secret from him the means of coercion at our disposal something that taints any love I show him? I speak to him kindly and with understanding, I endeavor to lighten his labors and praise them, I inquire earnestly as to his interests and thoughts, I make no shows of untoward anger against him, I consider aspects of his daily well-being, and yet I am aware of my own duplicity. It is for his own good, his own eternal good, I remind myself, and further, it is Satan who tries to persuade me otherwise, who causes me to indict my wise and politic course.

Yet my doubts recur and harass me.

9 January

I have awakened from a dream so revolting I scarcely dare commit it to paper. But if I am to have a proper record of this journey that I am embarked upon, which I now believe must have as much to do with my own soul's salvation as that of any other, I must.

In this dream I find myself with the Dumb One. He is of such rare beauty when he turns to look at me from his cook fire that I think he must have been transformed into an angel, and this is a transformation I remark to him, but he only smiles, an angelic smile, I think, and for no reason I kiss his lips. I kiss his lips again and we embrace arms and legs in close encounter and as we kiss eagerly many times I can feel the flutter of his wings, and the beating of the air, until I fall to earth and there is nothing there.

My first instinct upon awakening was to blame the Dumb One, as if it were he himself who was Satan. But it is not the Dumb One who has had this dream, it is I.

And I did not kiss his lips 'for no reason', as I just wrote. Dear God, I confess that I kissed them out of desire.

10 January

After the day's march I asked the Dumb One to leave the other men and come with me a distance, until, beyond a mild rise, we were out of sight and hearing of the others.

I brought with me the horsewhip, which may have caused him some consternation when he saw it. He looked at me as if asking whether he had done wrong. I said nothing.

It is possible Felipe or Ramon saw the whip in my hand when we left them, but I am not certain, and anyway there is no help for it. We are an intimate society. One takes such precautions as one can.

To his great surprise, when we were away from the others, I put the whip in his hand and commanded him to lash me.

He looked uncomprehending, the more so when I removed my garments to the waist.

His expression asked me why.

'Because I tell you to,' I said.

I half-expected his 'voice' to begin arguing with me then, but it did not.

From his expression I surmised that this was something he was extremely reluctant to do.

I placed myself on my knees. Physical processes have memories of their own, and I felt myself oddly close to prayer.

'Begin,' I ordered, knowing that if I did not say it, he never would.

His first stroke, I felt, was altogether weak. It was something still he was fearful to do.

I became angry with him. 'If you are as stupid and inept at this as at anything else, I will indeed find myself lashing you! Now do as you're told! Twenty, or till you get it right.'

But he got it right. He did indeed. He whipped me hard. With each lash I prayed to God that the pain would shoot straight to Satan's heart and drive him from me.

I felt I could hear the Dumb One weeping as he whipped me, but I dared not look.

When he was done he lifted me up and tenderly placed my garments on me. I could see there had indeed been tears in his eyes.

Before returning he picked some desert leaves and rubbed them lightly on my flesh, and they made a coolness that did indeed comfort.

I confess I wished for the Dumb One's voice then. I wished to hear it offering me human forgiveness.

10 January
later

Just now, as I watched the Dumb One sleep, I heard his voice. 'Your religion is strange,' it seemed to say. And then, as if to correct itself, 'Our religion is strange.'

How grateful I was to hear it, dear Lord. Yes, no matter the words, how grateful I was. Thanks be to You for not taking it from me.

Monterrey
12 January

We have arrived once again in Nuevo Leon. To my surprise I was informed that Fray Donaldo has been replaced. This apparently took place three months ago. Shipped off to Cartagena, a backwater destination if ever there was one. The new *custos* is Fray Antonio. I am not sure I like him any better than the last. For one thing, he has housed us less elegantly. We are no longer overlooking the cows, we are virtually among them. I would not call our lodgings a stable, but they are scarcely better.

Here I strive to remind myself of the circumstances of our Savior's birth. I avail myself of our Lord's example. I do not entirely succeed.

But beyond this peeve – exacerbated by the fact that I observed our former residence here, above the cow pond, and it is entirely unoccupied – I find this Fray Antonio's attitude even more hidebound than Fray Donaldo's.

It is as if they send all the hard men to Nuevo Leon, in recognition of its *converso* past. I drank Fray Antonio's dreadful wine, which tasted as if it had been made from the grape seeds, while he insisted to me that 'New Christians are simply different from you and me.'

'But are they different in superficial aspects, a different nose or color of eye, a difference in name or accent, or are they different in the only fundamental matter in this universe,' I reminded Fray Antonio, 'their capacity to let our Lord and Savior into their hearts and be saved?'

'Both,' he said, with I thought remarkable candor and even more remarkable cynicism. 'The baptism has not removed the curse.'

'In all?'

'I am speaking as a general matter. But if pressed to the wall, I would say yes, all.'

'We have a profound difference then,' I said to Fray Antonio. And I added, what I felt to be an excellent point: 'Even Saint Paul was a New Christian once.'

Fray Antonio poured me more wine, even while I tried to shield my glass from his attentions, and admitted that perhaps he had been hyperbolic. 'Well then let me have a go at your suspect, your mute,' he said. 'Perhaps he'll prove to me the error of my ways.'

'I'm not sure what you mean by "having a go" at him,' I said.

'Simply let me talk to him. You admit your own lack of pro-gress. Perhaps a different approach would bear fruit. And if it did, you would have won your point.'

At this, which combined cleverness and flattery in amounts more ample than I'd imagined the new *custos* of Monterrey to possess, I could hardly refuse. He will interview the Dumb One tomorrow. I've enjoined Fray Antonio to be respectful. I did not mention to him the Dumb One's voice, nor any of the fruits of my dialogues with it. Surely, dear God, it is a secret that You have bestowed on me alone, and if it is not, then I will soon enough hear about it from Fray Antonio.

13 January

Where to begin my record of this day of disasters? I was not present when Fray Antonio interviewed the Dumb One, nor did I speak with the Dumb One beforehand, either to warn him or otherwise. I felt I should leave their meeting in the hands of a fateful providence. One should not then, I suppose, place blame if the aftermath falls very far from what one desired.

I was to have dinner with Fray Antonio and other local church-men. The first indication I had of trouble was when Felipe came to me and reported that the Dumb One had not prepared the evening meal for the others and in fact was nowhere to be found.

I called for him hither and yon, to no avail. I then went directly to Fray Antonio. I asked him if he had detained my cook. He denied it. I then asked him how his discussion with the Dumb One had gone. He admitted that he had made little progress and called the Dumb One 'stiff-necked'.

'What did you talk about?' I asked. 'Did you question him as to his beliefs?'

'Of course, yes,' Fray Antonio said. 'But I'm afraid I was rather less accommodating than yourself. When he finally hid behind his muteness once too often, I alerted him in certain terms to the danger facing his immortal soul. I asked him if he really wanted to be like so many others of his type who undermine our holy edifice. I told him I did not believe that a *converso* could be trusted and that if it were up to me I would condemn them all. From his puzzlement I deduced that he hadn't a clue what I was speaking about. Really, Fray Alonso, have you kept him so in the dark? I told him that the Papal injunction against the Church shedding blood did not mean we had no means of dealing with the impenitent, and that if it were up to me I would relax him without delay to the secular authority. Again, I could not tell if he were playing the fool with me, but he seemed to have no idea what "relax" meant. He seemed to think it was something pleasant. Given his manifest ignorance, I felt I needed to enlighten him just a bit. So you'll forgive me, Fray Alonso, if I told him that for the Church to relax a heretic meant that we loosened our claim on him, we no longer shielded him or held hopes to reconcile him, we left him to his fate. The moron spread his hands as if asking for explanation. "What fate? I shall tell you, sir, what fate. The Church does not condone the shedding of blood," I repeated. "But when a man is burnt alive, his blood is not shed!" I could not lie to him, could I, Fray Alonso?' This last he uttered with an impish grin, the proof, I supposed, of his cruel hypocrisy.

'I asked you to be respectful with him!' I cried. 'I made it a condition of your interview!'

'It was he who had no respect for me, or for that matter you or all we stand for,' Fray Antonio said. 'He oughtn't to have got clever with me. I do not abide that.'

'And now he has run off!'

'I did find your decision not to bind him quite odd,' Fray Antonio said. 'I cannot be responsible for your negligent liberality.'

'I asked you to be respectful!'

'Please, there is no need for raised voices.'

'You have no idea the exigencies of our journey, the events that necessitated my decisions!'

'I am sure you had your reasons.'

'Where should I look for him?'

'I have no idea. I'm sorry.' Then, as I fled his presence, he called after me: 'I'm sure he'll show up someday. Probably as governor of the province, or the richest man in New Spain. It's how it goes with these people. I say, condemn them all!'

I caught a glimpse of his impudent grin once again.

I collected Felipe and Ramon and the three of us divided up

the town. Or I should say, its taverns and such, since we had no other idea where, if he remained in Monterrey at all, he might hide. My overwhelming suspicion was that he had fled the settlement altogether, that he had mounted one of the many trails out of town.

Monterrey, I should say, seems equally divided between respectable houses and houses of lesser repute. Indeed as a percentage of the whole, I doubt there are many municipalities that could boast as many brothels. We had much work to do, and were indeed failing at it, when at some time approaching the midnight hour, I was surprised to be accosted by a representative of Fray Antonio, who apparently had felt some remorse regarding his treatment of me and had sent out, without my knowledge, scouts to help in our endeavor. This one scout informed me that the Dumb One had been discovered, stinking drunk, in a house on the outskirts by the river.

I arrived presently at a house so destitute-looking and fragile that I could hardly imagine any sort of business, no less a profitably sinful one, taking place in its confines. All the brothels of Monterrey appear ramshackle, but this one barely stood up at all; an old, sway-backed donkey of a house with a curtain for a door and a lone window that looked to have been shoveled out of the adobe.

I found the Dumb One on the floor in a corner of this hut, guarded loosely by one of Fray Antonio's minions, whom I thanked and sent on his way. The Dumb One was curled in the dirt like a baby, with a woman whom I took to be the likely object of his recent affections bent over him with a pan of water, encouraging him to drink and receiving no response. She seemed to react warily to my clerical attire but then resumed her min-istrations, inserting a finger between the Dumb One's lips and pouring a few drips of water between them. The water for the most part splashed off his teeth and dribbled down his chin. I presumed she was only trying to revive him sufficiently to get him on his way. There were other men in the room, seated on chairs, and I supposed she and her colleagues were in the midst of a busy night.

I intervened to say that we would take him now. I ordered Felipe to help me lift him up. But when we commenced to do so, the woman grabbed at our arms, protesting loudly. 'Where are you taking him?' she cried. 'My husband! He's my husband now!'

'He was a single man when we saw him earlier today,' I opined.

'My husband! Don't take him!' she went on.

But take him we did, on the assumption that the girl's protests were one sort of ruse or other, perhaps deployed in the hope that the Dumb One had money that might later be robbed from him. I even said to the girl, in the sort of rude pidgin I imagined she would understand, 'No money. Poor man. Do not worry about it.' And Ramon pried her fingers off our arms, and then off the Dumb One's legs, to which she momentarily clung, and we took him outside, whereat, by the riverbank, Felipe found a cart to hire, and we dumped the Dumb One in this cart and directed its owner to return him to our quarters.

Our surprise came only when the Dumb One awakened. He appeared distraught. His eyes scoured the room and he made a very delicate, cupped motion with his hand, as if caressing a face. We were now back in our rooms, where I had been preparing to record the day's events in this very journal. I was inordinately stern with him. I hardly found it appropriate that my captive, given freedom by my own grace, should take the first opportunity to go whoring. I berated him for his foolishness and wantonness. But he was only mildly impressed by my tongue-lashings. He kept looking around as if for someone.

'Who are you looking for?' I demanded.

He again made that very delicate, cupped motion with his hand.

And the voice, the Dumb One's voice, uttered to my mind: 'Felicia.'

'You're looking for that whore, whose name is Felicia?' I said aloud.

He shook his head one way then the other, assenting and denying.

'What are you saying?'

I scrutinized his helpless confusion.

Then his voice 'spoke' again. 'She is not a whore anymore. She's my wife.'

'Oh, she's your wife, is she now? And how long have you been married? Two hours? Three?'

He nodded vigorously.

'And when did you meet? An hour before that?'

He again nodded vigorously.

'And who married you? A priest? Which priest?'

But his nods now changed to equally vigorous denials.

'If not a priest, then who?'

His helpless look, his sly, seductive, deceptive look of inno-cence, which I had fallen for so many times.

And I heard his voice say, 'Married by love.'

So there it was. As had become my invariable habit, I passed the words back to him for confirmation. 'You were married by love? Love married you?'

Yes, yes, yes.

Who but a Dumb One, I suppose I wondered. Married 'by love' alone!

Yet I imagine I would have forgiven all of it, the running off, the whoring, the drunken foolishness. After all, I was convinced that Fray Antonio had provoked him. But the day was not done with its sad surprises. Indeed, it had saved the worst revelation for the last.

Fray Antonio, accompanied by two of the men whom he had sent out as scouts, appeared solemnly at our door. I expressed my surprise at his still being awake at this hour.

'It is not my preference,' he humorlessly allowed. 'Do you have your cook with you?'

'I do.'

'May I come in?'

The three men strode past me, to face the Dumb One as he lay on the bed of straw from which he had awakened.

'What is this about?' I asked.

Fray Antonio drew from within his vest a small censer of silver plate. 'Ask him where this came from,' he said to me.

I was taken aback by the lack of context, but sensing the atmosphere of suspicion, I asked the Dumb One, 'Do you know what he is talking about? Do you know where this came from?'

His eyes moved from mine to the censer, which Fray Antonio held before him, swinging in the stagnant air of our room like a clock's pendulum.

The Dumb One indicated neither one thing nor the other. His eyes, bulging, rested on me again like weights.

'Let me fill in the story then,' Fray Antonio said, with a triumphant air which I loathed but could hardly deny him. 'This censer, of modest but honest value, properly belongs to the Chapel of Our Lady that adjoins my offices, but was tonight found in that stinking sewer of sin in which our philosopher-cook here was also found. He had used it, no doubt, to purchase the services of one of the resident strumpets...' But he got no further in his indictment because the Dumb One leapt at Fray Antonio, whereupon all of us, myself, Fray Antonio, his so-called 'scouts', Felipe and Ramon, intervened to restrain him. It required very nearly all our collective strength to do so.

And so I am brought to a low point in my hopes for this wicked man. I can blame Fray Antonio and his provocations all I wish, but a theft remains a theft, and much worse still is a theft from a consecrated place. Above all, I fault my failure of perception. There were flaws in this Dumb One that I did not contemplate. I will now pray for his soul, but with greater wariness.

You whose grace and mercy granted me the miracle of this sinner's 'voice' so that I might lead him to Your fold, or so that I might find instead the humility of failure, grant me the wisdom to know one from the other and the heart to accept whichever shall be. I pray for greater love, I pray for the Dumb One's soul.

Tomorrow we depart for the capital.

THE POUCH

Entries from 16 January 1650 to 1 March 1650

en route
16 January

I have removed those privileges which I had previously granted the Dumb One. He is again tied to a tree at night. On taking such action, I was aware that I might be creating a sullen passenger. This did not distress me. What distressed me was the enormous effort I had expended in fruitless pursuit of his ultimate well-being.

Last night I had a frank talk with him, while he was tied to his tree. 'Listen here, Juan,' I said, and he had to know that my use of his Christian name bore no glad tidings for him, 'Fray Antonio must have explained to you the possible consequences of your continued obstinacy. Perhaps he was not the perfect messenger, but I am here to tell you that all that he said to you about fateful consequences is correct. You shall burn in Hell if you remain unrepentant to your God, and you shall burn on earth, in a place, yes, set aside for just such unrepentant ones, in the City of Mexico, before that. Have you perhaps not heard of the *quemadero?* It is a place of last resort, but it is nonetheless a place. I have tried to shield you from such frightful possibilities on the assumption that one as clever as yourself, who had perhaps been but the victim of unfortunate origins, would recognize the great truths I have attempted to inculcate. But now my doubts give way to righteous rage! You shall burn, sir, and I shall not blink an eye, if you continue on this path!

'It is not a question of this evil befalling you,' I continued. 'It is a question of curing you of evil. It is an awful thing to burn a man. But the very thought of it inspires fear, and fear may be efficacious, when no other options remain, when a man cherishes untruth and resists every other option that might save him.'

The Dumb One made no answer to any of this. He looked at me with a somewhat doe-eyed confusion, or perhaps it was wonderment, and held his peace.

I then referred to the fact that he was again bound up. 'I feel this will put us on an honest footing,' I said.

To my surprise, the Dumb One's 'voice' made an appearance. 'Agreed,' it said without words.

'Is that so? You agree with me?' I asked the Dumb One directly. He nodded that he did. I must say, I was not prepared for such mildness on his part.

I took the opportunity to ask what explanation he might supply for his theft from a church.

The 'voice' again answered, and the Dumb One then

confirmed: 'My wife is so poor. I thought she must have something. One little thing. I know stealing is bad. Could Satan cloud my mind?'

'He certainly could!' I thundered aloud.

'Then you will understand it this way,' the voice quietly answered.

'But how do *you* understand it?' I asked wordlessly.

'I'm sorry to cause you trouble. You've been kind to me,' the voice answered.

'Are you sorry to God?' I asked wordlessly.

'You will understand it that way,' the voice said.

Later the voice came to me in my sleep. It was the first time it had done so. It seemed to say, 'I did it' – and by this I understood he meant his theft from the church – 'so you would know I am only a man.'

23 *January*

For some days I have neglected this journal, as our progress has been easy and regular. Having hired two new men in Monterrey, I can now declare that they work well. The hunter among them, Raoul, is a passable substitute for Alberto. The weather has been dry, the trail well-marked and easy. I feel as if we have returned to settled territory, even when days pass and we see no other human beings.

In recent days I have observed that the Dumb One, no sooner has he scrubbed out the cookware and bowls, and submitted to his leg being bound, retreats into scratching in the dirt with whatever stick might be within his reach. I have observed this strange habit for some days at a distance. Tonight I approached him, as if to start a conversation, but really out of curiosity. I could see that he was drawing something in the earth. 'Your philosophy?' I asked with, I suppose, a mixture of jauntiness and mild sarcasm.

He stopped his scratching and regarded me with either earnestness or blankness. He appeared to me tired. More than the journey was exhausting him. I presumed it was my harsh words of days before or the prospects that those words, and Fray Antonio's, had opened for him.

But now I could see what he was doing in the dirt. In altogether primitive fashion, like a child whose few simple lines convey all the sense of the world it possesses, he was making pictures of a girl.

'Felicia… Your "wife"?'

He paused a moment, and then resumed his work. I watched him for a period. It was a night of full moon and the sandy dirt darkly sparkled. His lines were as clear as if he were etching them in stone. He hesitated, added a stroke or two, hesitated again, added again. But he scratched nothing out. Soon enough he had drawn several 'Felicias' in the sand, happy Felicias, sad Felicias, Felicias who appeared lost and confused, hopeful Felicias.

They were banal, of course, every one of them. No matter. I

was touched, despite myself. There was a purity to all of this, the scene, his meager stick in the dirt, the hopelessness of this love that I myself had taken from him.

For of course I had not imagined the Dumb One 'in love' at all. I had imagined only that he had satisfied his lust, paid for it with stolen coin, and that was the end of it. Lust, I'd imagined, was all he was capable of, and he had confused it with love.

But his drawings in the sand were not lustful. It is hardly an area of my expertise, dear God, but I believe the notion 'first love' applies. The Dumb One, as I now understand it, frightened by Fray Antonio into believing he was headed for the stake, sought out a common whore so that he would not die without having known a woman. But, simple soul that he was, this woman he knew first, however simple herself, however fallen, became like the world to him. And continues to be. A story as banal as his sketches, and yet I am moved.

And to think, unless You will it, she will never know these tokens of love he draws every night in the earth.

I offered him paper. I said surely we should be able to find a few scraps, I even imagined I would tear a few pages from this journal, but he refused.

'She hears me anyway,' his 'voice' told my mind.

A love outside the Church, a love I do not condone. And yet, why do I not sense it as evil?

Today I have been plagued by the following meditation: regardless of the Dumb One's heresies, he is of no danger to anyone but himself and so would I ever have bothered to pursue him except for the pricks of my own ambition? The thought of returning to the capital with not a single suspect – is it not this that drives me more than anything? That somehow Fray Luis, or perhaps even the Inquisitor General himself, would be able to pin my failure not on the pathetic misdirection of my mission, but on my own shortcomings? A single mangy country fool would hardly turn that judgment around, but he would be better than nothing at all. Again: is this why I persecute the Dumb One? And if this is why, is it not an unworthy motive, one that I must purge from myself and only then ask whether my suspicions of him are just?

It is a fear that has plagued me all day, doubtless brought about by the touching effects of seeing the Dumb One so helplessly, indeed one might even say close to innocently, in love.

It is only tonight that I have resolved my worry, in recollecting that Satan constantly puts obstacles in our path. Men's motives are never pure, not mine nor any man's. If we wait for perfection from such poor instruments as ourselves before acting, our Holy Church will surely fall and with it man's lifeline to God. I hereby confess that I am ambitious, self-interested, fearful, venal, cowardly and often unkind, but I shall purify my instrument as best I can and not be deterred.

28 January

Another conversation that took place in silence between the Dumb One and myself, while he slept with a frightful snore by his tree. I could not sleep myself, both for his snoring and for assorted worries.

'My ancestor rode with Coronado,' his 'voice' told my mind.

'You have previously told me this,' I wordlessly said, and then chose to humor him. 'My own ancestor rode with Cortes.'

'What was his name?' the voice asked.

'Don Federico de la Ronda,' I wordlessly said.

'Mine was Don Tomas Rodrigues de Santangel,' the voice said.

'I know. You have told me,' I wordlessly replied.

'Perhaps they knew each other. Your ancestor and my ancestor,' the voice said.

'I regret to inform you, sir,' I said, 'that Cortes lived an entire century before Coronado.'

'In spirit. They could know each other in spirit,' the voice said.

'Or in God,' I said, and to this the voice made no reply.

3 February

After we quit our march for today, I approached the Dumb One at his cook station and, after suitable courtesies, asked him a simple yes-or-no question, which summarized the meditations that have been troubling my mind on and off since the night I found him drawing in the dirt. 'If by telling me a lie, you could gain your freedom and run off to see this Felicia, would you do so?'

He answered nothing at all.

I took a more accusatory tone with my second question: 'Would you not lie to me right now? Would you not lie even in answer to my previous question, or to this very one, if by so doing you could procure your freedom and your "love"?'

His eyes chilled and avoided mine. He turned his back to me, went to one of the mule packs of our provisions, withdrew from it something I did not immediately see, and came back to his cook fire, which he then attended with concentrated interest. In a few moments I saw that what he had taken from the pack was a candle, which he now lit from the campfire and placed with melted wax on one of the stones that attended his work. It was not yet evening. And today is Friday.

On seeing this vast arrogance, or indifference, or whatever it was, this outrage, really, I curtailed myself and asked, in an unraised voice, why he had lit this candle even in my presence.

I received no answer. Indeed, he made a conscious display of ignoring me, cupping the candle till the flame was strong, returning then to the cook fire. What a busy man he had suddenly become!

Nor did his reliable 'voice' return to my mind.

Maintaining my self-control, I went to the mule pack from which the Dumb One had withdrawn the candle, searched the compartment he had opened, and discovered there a dozen or so more small candles. I seized them all.

'Your incorrigibility does not serve you well,' I said.

Tears. He displayed tears! At which I lost the smallest part of my composure and, with a gesture that was more a swipe than a simple reach, grabbed the lit candle on its stone and dropped it in the cook fire.

'No more of this, shall we?' I said tightly.

There were still tears in his eyes, which I hated him for.

4 February

The judaizing instinct runs strong and deep. What else explains why in my very presence he would light the sabbath candle? It runs so deep, apparently, that those in whom it runs may not even know it is doing so. Surely this is the case with this Dumb One. I must somehow persuade him of the dark habit he carries, and that, if I may surmise, leads to strange other aspects of his thought. How is it that the ancient leaden prescriptions of Judaism lead to free thinking? It seems unlikely enough, yet the proof of it is before my eyes!

If I were made to guess, the *Marrano* in his family, if there was only one, was this very conquistador of whom he is so proud. The historical record is plain that *conversos* sailed with all our Hispanic Majesties' great seaward expeditions, they were already with Cortes, they were with Pizarro and Ponce de León, they were even essential to the great Columbus, so why should they not also have ridden with Coronado?

12 February

So little of anything eventful has happened to us over these past days that I have begun to meditate on the inconsequence of all that I do. Am I not a forgotten speck in the vastness of this wasteland? In truth, the Holy Church may prevail or stumble, the great nations joust and fall, and all that happens, happens without regard to my infinitely paltry actions. Is this self-pity speaking? Is this Satan speaking? Or is it only a recognition of the truth?

These vast desiccations, this endless wilderness: they stir the soul, but to what end?

I think of Your earliest followers, in their desert retreats. I think then, in turn, of my Dumb One, alive in similar places. What lesson applies?

I have again begun to be fearful, as if threatened by an awful nothingness.

I pray that You not forget Your sinful, prideful servant.

I make confession, as well, that the Dumb One's ample and well-cooked meals have been not without consolation. For days we have been dining on a slain elk, variously and ingeniously prepared by him. At meal times, we are like lion cubs at a mother's kill.

14 February

This night past I was awakened by a coyote's howling. I lay awake with the stars, trying to penetrate with my eyes and heart their infinitude. Only when I shut my eyes did I begin to pray, and continued to pray until the morning.

1 March

The sun returned, after several days of rain, and we had an excellent, swift march, in celebration of which I authorized the opening of some skins of wine. I was thinking, as well, that the men could use some cheering up.

And lo, having passed one of the skins to the Dumb One even as he was tied to his tree for the night, I observed that he had become quite drunk. It must be that he is unused to drink.

I tried to start one of my 'conversations' with him, but he was presently incapable of even a coherent shake of his head.

And then he fell asleep. Or more accurately, he was passed clear out, his torso splayed on the ground, his head leaned up against his tree without rigor, like a flower that has drooped. I first nudged him to see if there was any point to attempting further monologue. He barely budged and emitted a snore. It was only when I attempted this one or two times more, without success in rousing him, that a further plot proposed itself to me.

'Juan, Juan,' I called him by name. Still nothing. I could see the slight bulge that the leather pouch that hung from his neck made underneath his tunic. Indeed my eyes, rather involuntarily, began increasingly to focus on that very bulge. It was as if some primordial prosecutorial instinct were whispering to me, 'The proof, the proof, there it may be!'

And I calculated further that this might be my only chance, since under ordinary conditions of sleep, with the dangers of the trail lightening all our slumbers, it seemed unlikely that I could loosen so close a possession to his body without him knowing it and awakening.

I tried several times just to tickle his neck and to pull his tunic slightly down from it, as if to test him. His breath stank heavily of the wine and he showed no sign of consciousness.

Finally I did that deed which duty and curiosity in equal parts were commending me to do. As the Dumb One lay there, I lifted the worn leather pouch out from his tunic and loosened the tie which tied it shut, and with great gentleness inserted my two fingers therein, until I felt a single sheet of paper, that appeared well-folded.

I lifted the paper from its historic womb, fully expecting to find on it that backward and strange Hebraic lettering which appears as if it had come directly from some other, and super-ceded, world. Yes, the Hebrew writing would be my proof! I would at last have something to challenge him with, to confront him with, to hold over him in the name of faith. Or, if needs be, to condemn him.

When I opened the crisply-folded paper, I was shocked to dis-cover that the foreign language it was written in was not Hebrew, but Latin. I understood the text immediately.

It was the Dumb One's certificate of baptism.

THE TORTURE

Entries from 2 March 2 1650 to 19 April 1650

2 March

And so, far from having proof of his judaizing, I have evidence that the Dumb One's mother wished that he be able to prove himself a Christian.

But what does that mean, really? She could have wished it so that he would have a cover for his secret practices. After all, every *Marrano* did convert. If they had not converted, the Church would not have the very problem that our Holy Office was instituted to deal with. If there were only Jews and no *conversos,* our Inquisition would have neither purpose nor subjects.

Though would a simple woman be so calculating?

But how do I know she was a simple woman?

By her son's own admission, she was lettered.

And did she not produce a son who may deceive by his very ability to appear undeceiving?

... Or is it only I, by virtue of my profession, and not the Dumb One or his mother, who walk in this hall of mirrors?

City of Mexico
14 March

At last! The past evening we camped within sight of the cathedral's spires, and today, in the morning hours, entered the city. I recall the myriad occasions when I imagined never seeing the capital again.

Yet it does not excite great fondness in me to be here. Rather here than on the road, but rather elsewhere altogether than here. To see the modest achievements of the city is for me a reminder of all that I have read must be greater across the ocean. My thoughts of such places and things are surely a recipe for eternal discontent, and hardly something to be praised, but on the other hand I don't suppose it is the worst sin to dream of finer things.

Or is it, dear Lord? Do I go too easy on my casual greed? Do I confess only half the sinner?

A humble heart. This is what I must at every instant, with every fiber of my strength, strive for.

Everywhere I turn, even in my pious confession, I find my relentless pride.

As opposed to my tepid response, I must note the reactions of the Dumb One to our capital. To him, every block of modest houses or shops is a marvel. The number of people on the streets, a kind of miracle. 'Open-mouthed', 'wide-eyed'; these all too familiar phrases do indeed convey the sense of wonder in him as we made our way to the center. I confess it did not displease me to be his guide. I felt a bit like the city mouse showing the country mouse. Perhaps also I felt the pleasure, had I been a parent, that I might have experienced showing my son the things of this world. The hanging gardens, the Royal Indian Hospital, the Zocalo and Cathedral, the palaces of government and administration, the canals and tree-lined parks, the avenues, even the pathetic heaps of heathen ruins, all appeared to excite in him a sense that his life previously had been modest by comparison. I fain hope that my motive in showing him all these was not simply to pleasure him or excite envy in him or play the braggart, but rather to instill in him my conviction that the life he has lived hitherto has been wanting in many respects, that just as the civilization here is greater than what he has known, so the truths of religion and philosophy to be found here are greater than those he now holds.

Even the Plazuela del Volador excited his wonder. I spoke softly to him there, saying, 'There is the *quemadero*, there is the place of our Holy Faith's last recourse, which all decent, pious men loathe yet hold in awe. It has apparently been idle since the great *Auto* of the past spring, which without a doubt persuaded many on wrongful paths to amend their ways, to their eternal benefit. Now ordinary men and women, even children, pass it by with scarcely a glance, as if it were a market on other than market-day, or the statue of Cortes that has become a magnet for the crows' expulsions.

At half past noon, after this period of seeing the sights, I delivered him to Fray Jorge d'Aranda, who remains, despite rumors of a new assignment in Lima that like my own hopes have received little confirmation, the warden of our Holy Office. Fray Jorge greeted me cordially, and we chatted for a time about the desolate conditions to the north. He once made a similar journey, to El Paso del Norte, and he joked that he was still recovering from it. 'What have we here?' he asked at last, turning to regard the Dumb One as if he were a prime lamb coming in to auction.

I suggested to him that the Dumb One was a decent sort who had yet managed to acquire, and by dint of stubbornness maintain, certain dangerous and questionable beliefs which I had confidence the vast resources of the capital might be able to dissuade him from. I asked Fray Jorge to treat him decently and as much like a guest as conditions allowed. Fray Jorge said, 'He's a fine-looking lad, I'll give him that. What a pity! Has he no speech whatsoever?' Then he addressed the Dumb One directly: 'You'd have a far nicer accommodation in this city if you'd allow Fray Alonso here to talk some sense into you. Fray Alonso, I'll tell you, son, knows good sense more than anybody.'

I thanked Fray Jorge, with a facetiousness more sincere than it sounded, for his commendation.

As the warden and I spoke, the Dumb One stared fixedly at the iron gates that loomed in front of him, and the narrow passage beyond. I must confess, the sober impression was not other than what I felt ought to be made on him. The man must come to his senses!

Before I abandoned him to the warden's custody, I left the Dumb One with these words: 'In the event I have falsely suspected you, sir, I apologize now for both past and future. But if you do stand falsely accused, please know that your sufferings until such time as your innocence can be proved will be as a martyrdom to the Faith, since the process in which you are now embroiled, imperfect as it may be in this case or that, including I confess yours perhaps, is one nevertheless without which the scores of millions of souls in our Holy Church's care would be in mortal danger.'

Of course, I say something like that to every suspect.

'I will come to visit you very soon,' I said to the Dumb One, and went out.

3 *March*

My great relief of the day is to have discovered that the voyage of the *Suprema*'s emissary, whom I despaired of seeing when sent on my journey, has been delayed for many months, so that the Inquisitor General now anticipates his arrival in the next fortnight. What a stroke! Apparently the ship he initially booked passage on sunk in a squall while approaching Cádiz, and so all his plans were delayed. The same winds that must needs have been so horrific and fateful for many are thus a boon to me. God is good and merciful, but also complicated. I shall have my chance to present my case for a transfer in person after all!

I learned all this during my dinner with the Inquisitor General himself. We enjoyed a fine meal of pheasant and port at the refectory. He seemed in excellent spirits, welcoming me back to the fold with jokes and claps on the back. Things have been quiet around here. Apparently the great *Auto* of last year did indeed have the effect I expected. The Inquisitor General's fear now is that due to the paucity of suspects (in itself due to our excellence in reforming the colony) a reduction in our budget might be in the offing. 'Thus it is possible we have succeeded too well,' he lamented. Under these circumstances, my own meager prisoner, my Dumb One, was not regarded by him with as much contempt as I had anticipated.

It was left to Fray Luis, of course, to deflate my achievement. He stopped by our table, looking lean and ambitious as ever. I have decided there is something in his appearance I particularly detest – his eyebrows. The way they descend toward his nose, almost swooping, their thickness and the sharpness of their curve; in sum they remind me of some scavenging bird. He engaged me in the customary niceties that always cause my shoulders to stiffen, awaiting his next maneuver. I did not have to wait long. 'Quite a catch you've brought us!' he proclaimed cheerily. 'I can't wait to sink my teeth into his defense.'

'You?' I asked, astonished.

'For six months, Fray Luis has been our new advocate for the accused,' the Inquisitor General said.

'I simply got tired of pesos and account books,' Fray Luis suggested innocently.

'But you'll have no dealings with him, I don't suppose, unless there is actually a formal case,' I said.

What I meant to imply was for him to keep hands off the

Dumb One, but I regretted my words immediately, which sounded defensive and unsure.

'Are you saying it's a weak case against him?' Fray Luis asked cheerfully. 'That's a pity then. I was hoping you would be bringing me more work.'

'Well you could hardly expect it, given the fool's errand I was sent on,' I said. And I regretted these testy words of mine as well.

Fray Luis has simply a way of getting my goat. And this new assignment of his! How else can I interpret it but as a career move? To know all aspects of the Office, to move around as quickly as possible, to present oneself as prepared to assume any and all responsibility! Well, I shall not compete with that. I don't care to. All I long for is to leave this place! Regarding which, in the person of the *Suprema's* emissary, I still have hopes that my ship may be coming. And soon.

Before moving off to his own table, Fray Luis rubbed my shoulder in a manner meant to seem collegial, but which I felt as repugnant and presumptuous. 'I suppose I should be glad no longer to have the treasury as my concern. You didn't exactly bring us back a millionaire, Fray Alonso!'

And he was off. From then on, the pheasant tasted dry in my mouth. I would like to report that the Inquisitor General made some remark or other to undermine my ridiculous adversary's pretensions. But he did not. He even laughed at that jest about the money.

No matter how one looks at it, I have brought back a minnow. This is hardly a surprise to me. Yet I continue to be distressed, not by my failure, but by the fact that it can be considered a failure! And even by myself! I recognize Fray Luis's jest! But is not every soul precious? If every soul is not precious, then we, we Inquisitors, indeed our Holy Office, have no right to exist! We are not here to acquiesce in the world's fall.

Brave words. How shall I back them up?

5 *March*

I visited the Dumb One in his cell of incarceration, which is no more dank and fetid than any other, which is to say very dank and fetid indeed. In times past, on every occasion I paid such a prison visit, I felt a welling of the sin of pride, that it was not I who was so deprived, not I who stood suspected of horrific crime, not I who had been humiliated. After each occasion I would confess my sin, but my confession did not prevent its recurrence the next time. Today I felt only pity.

The Dumb One sat on the stone floor as if he intended to outwait his life. There appeared no hope in him, but no desperation either. He did not mock me, nor accuse me for winding him up in this place. Instead he looked at my full arms as if to ask me what I had brought him.

'Books,' I said. 'I thought I might read to you.'

I sat down beside him on the chilled floor and showed him Aquinas, in Spanish of course, and Saint Augustine, and a book concerning Saint Francis. I thought our beloved Franciscan founder might have particular appeal to him, and so read to him for quite a while, my intention being to show him that, as I put it upon concluding, 'It is possible to know and love nature and also be a Christian.'

The Dumb One regarded me blankly. Once again I had no idea of his thoughts, until the 'voice' that for many days had been absent, to the point where I had even come to miss it and hope for its return, appeared in my mind.

'I am a Christian,' it said.

'Of course you are,' I said wordlessly. 'But you need to be a better Christian.'

'Is a better Christian made by force?' he asked. Ah, his pet argument again, his hobby-horse, which he will ride, I do not doubt, all the way to Hell.

'Of course not,' I patiently rejoined in my mind. 'Force can only be a reminder.'

'A reminder does not keep me from my wife. Walls do. Locks and keys. Force.'

I said aloud to the Dumb One, 'I will come again soon and read to you some more. I pray you reflect. The force you refer to is the force that can be applied to a body. Bodies can be forced. But souls cannot.'

I got off the floor to leave.

He did not appear perturbed. Indeed, I felt, however oddly, that he welcomed my visit but would welcome the resumption of his solitude as well.

'Your situation may be more dire than I had even previously

imagined,' I said. 'If you end up accused and must be put on trial, your advocate will be a man I do not trust, and would urge you not to trust either.'

And so I left him.

7 March

Because of my involvement in discovering and arresting the Dumb One, the Inquisitor General has informed me, as I fully expected, that my further involvement in the case, in the formal sense, will be confined to being a witness. As such, today I gave my deposition. Having refreshed my memory with these journal pages, I was able to testify with great accuracy as to dates, chronologies, *et cetera*. I was also able to admit into testimony several highly favorable reflections on the Dumb One's character, his courage in the face of savage attack, his care for the sick, his mildness of manner. At the same time, I omitted any reference to the Dumb One's 'voice'. This is my private insight. It would of course be inadmissible at trial. It might even serve to impeach me: Fray Luis might use it to suggest that I was quite mad!

The prosecution of the matter has been assigned to Fray Sebastian de San Martin, the very colleague who gifted me with this journal, and whose reputation as a fair and relentless *promotor fiscal* is unimpeachable.

8 March

But what if I am quite mad? What if it is neither God nor Satan who brings the Dumb One's words into my head, what if 'his' words begin and end in the chambers of my mind? To hear voices. Isn't this where madness begins?

I remind myself, with greatest urgency, how often and how unfailingly the Dumb One has confirmed the meanings conveyed in his 'voice.' There, on the delicate strands of those confirmations, lies the proof of my sobriety. There lies my proof of You.

13 March

Fray Sebastian has indeed shown he means business. Today, less than one week after my deposition, he issued his *clamosa*. The charge against the Dumb One: judaizing. Fray Sebastian has apparently decided to treat the various philosophical affirmations made by the Dumb One in answer to my inquiries as merely the opinions of an untutored simpleton. The lighting of sabbath candles is another matter entirely. This is the sole allegation he must prove for a conviction.

I must say I admire Fray Sebastian's prosecutorial cleverness in thus framing the indictment. Everything that might be excused by insanity, or shaded into mootness and ambiguity by advocacy, he has eliminated. All he needs show are a few simple facts. And in my deposition he plainly believes he has them.

Indeed, we spoke briefly after the *clamosa* was issued. We had not seen one another, outside the formal setting of the deposition room, since my departure. He inquired quite graciously of my welfare and my various adventures. I went so far as to put in, so to say, a 'good word' for the Dumb One on a personal basis, while emphasizing to Fray Sebastian my profound hopes for reconciling him to the Church's bosom. As any good *promotor fiscal* should be regarding a case he is now prosecuting, Fray Sebastian was noncommittal as regards my personal musings.

17 March

I have decided, due to the nice coincidence of it being Fray Sebastian who gifted me with this journal, and to the fact I can now count the blank pages remaining and they are none too many, to devote what space remains here primarily to recording the case of the Dumb One, which has so fascinated me and absorbed my concern. In doing so, I recognize that I am no more than confirming a species of obsession which my scribbling in these pages already largely reflects.

26 March

Today I received a message by way of the warden, Fray Jorge, that the Dumb One would like to see me. I put aside my long-overdue attentions to the Holy Office's tulip garden and proceeded shortly to the prison, thinking I would read to him from Aquinas but in truth possessing no fresh strategy with which to approach his obstinacy. I entertained vague hopes that the issuance of the *clamosa* might at minimum have focused his attention on the seriousness of his circumstances.

On entering the dank and darkened cell that has become his worldly extent, I observed that the Dumb One, like some rare flower that profits from the darkness, has taken on a comeliness in his confinement. He was always a good-looking, open-faced lad, but now the adverse conditions he suffers, or perhaps in particular his failure to eat properly, have given his face a proper intensity. He is all dark eyes and brows, his cheeks thin manfully but do not sink, his lips, moistened by hunger, yet have a serenity that does not so much defeat desire as overlay it. In short, his sufferings mature him; he has left the awkwardness of youth behind.

'Have you been treated adequately?' I asked him at the outset, and he nodded that he had. 'Have you been eating?' Another nod, albeit rather less enthusiastic. 'And you are aware of the indictment that has been issued?' Once again, his assent.

'So. Did you call for me because you had something to tell me, or did you wish for me to read to you again?... Read to you again? No? Then did you have something to say to me? Yes?'

His expression drooped, until, to my surprise he appeared sheepish. He hung his head and his stricken eyes reached up towards me like the scarred hands of a beggar.

'What is it?'

His 'voice' answered: 'I did not mean to insult you or your beliefs. I'm grateful for your honest treatment of me. I am sorry.'

So shocked was I by this apology that I repeated every word that I had 'heard' back to the Dumb One. He affirmed that this was how he felt. And I understood one thing further, which must be so: he had missed me.

Dear Holy Father, I felt I saw my chance to serve You.

'Has your lawyer come to see you?' I asked.

Yes, the Dumb One affirmed, Fray Luis had come.

'And did he tell you that the indictment had to do with lighting candles?'

Yes, he had said this.

'Did he tell you any more?'

The Dumb One shook his head no.

'So he did not tell you, as I've told you many times, that lighting a candle on Friday evenings is a Jewish rite which our Holy Church cannot allow to Christians? You do this wantonly, brazenly, as if you fail to see the fault in it. But I tell you, here and now, that to be reconciled to the Church, you need to admit your fault and guilt and repent. You must admit it is wrong, and that you know it is wrong, and even that you know why it is wrong, because it is judaizing, and unbelief, and you repent of it.'

He looked at me with that ghost-like innocence of his, shadowed in the cell's dankness. It was midday out in the world he was scarcely still part of, and the smallest shard of light from the window-slit made of his face a kind of portrait of... what? Grief? Confusion? Earnest and chaste love?

Or did his face perhaps only reflect mine?

'It is my testimony on which the indictment is based. You know that, don't you?'

He nodded that he knew that.

'I will always come here if you ask. How does that suit you? I promise you I will come. Because I am waiting... I think you know for what.'

I then read him several pages from the great Aquinas. He did not seem impressed. Perhaps he did not even comprehend.

Dear God, what a wretched instrument of Yours I am! One simple, parched, desert fool, on whom if I could but pour a few drops of Your truth he would surely bloom, and yet I am incapable of it!

And now, many hours later, when I record this, what do I feel? Pity, I suppose. Pity which I know the others, Fray Sebastian or the Inquisitor General or Fray Jorge or, surely, Fray Luis, do not feel. For all of them, he is just another case. A set of facts, a collection of evidence, an accusation to be proved or not. And why should it be otherwise? When has it ever been otherwise? I have been part of this Office thirteen years and it has never been otherwise, even with me.

Yet I feel pity. As if the charge against this man, while true enough, and the result of my own hand, yet does not match his heart. Or, as I would like to say, his Christian heart.

7 April

The interrogation of the Dumb One by Fray Sebastian commenced on Monday morning and continued, mornings only, through the week. I wish I could report some fireworks or dramatic revelations which might have punctuated the proceedings, but, on the contrary, my strongest impression has been an abiding sense of lethargy. Fray Sebastian's questions are generally *pro forma*, crafted out of my deposition into simple yes-or-no inquiries, and the Dumb One's nods or denials as the case may be are duly recorded. Fray Luis sits by the Dumb One's side and makes no objections, and I learn nothing that I did not know before and have not previously recorded in this very journal.

The most interesting observations I can make regard the Dumb One himself, who from the first seemed impressed by the grandeur and trappings of the Tribunal hall, as if he were surprised we would take so much trouble for the likes of himself. It is almost as if he'd not previously been aware of his own importance. He looks at everything around him, the balustrades, the ornaments, the refinements on the Inquisitor General's robes, with a curiosity bordering on fascination. There are even moments when he seems to be enjoying himself. I am still not certain he fathoms the consequences of all this. Of course he is aware of them, he has by now often been told them, but I am not sure he believes them. Then too, he must be pleased to be out of his cell. As for the others, the assigned representatives of the Holy Office, I sometimes feel the midday meal is uppermost in their minds. Everyone but the Dumb One himself seems aware that this is a low-level case.

I myself have been allowed to be present, though I have no official part, by the Inquisitor General's dispensation, in view of my long and intimate concern with the matter and the fact that I am a deposed witness. I sit in the rear and from time to time attract the Dumb One's glances. They are never pleading, nor even inquisitive. I am simply of interest to him, as is everything else. Or anyway, this is my interpretation.

The proceedings have moved in a predictable course. Fray Sebastian has quite properly established that the Dumb One lights sabbath candles as his mother did before him, that he expresses no remorse for doing so, and that he denies any judaizing intention. It would of course be the easiest thing in the world for the Dumb One to reverse the dire trajectory of the evidence by renouncing himself and expressing penitence. But he has shown no sign of doing so, and Fray Luis sits back in his chair throughout.

It is as if I and I alone am aware that a soul hangs in the balance. If the Dumb One must ultimately go to the *quemadero*, so be it and may God have mercy on him. But what I cannot continue to abide is the indifference of all concerned.

On a brighter note, I have learned that the ship carrying the *Suprema's* emissary docked at Veracruz nine days ago. It shall thus be only a matter of days or short weeks before his appearance here. May the Lord speed his safe journeying, so that it may be very nearly as rapid as the news of him. I confess to quivers of anticipation.

9 April

Last night I prayed continuously that the efforts of our Holy Office be purified and its corruptions be expunged. But how can I cast stones at others when I find my every fifth thought going towards the wonders of Seville, the marvels of Córdoba, the day of the emissary's arrival? Holy Father, I am as worldly as any of them, once my depths are plumbed. Or is the plainer fact that I have no depths?

Fray Luis floored me this morning with the prediction that he would soon clear the Dumb One of all charges against him. This took place outside the chapel, where Fray Luis was making his 'cheery', gossipy rounds. 'And how shall you achieve that?' I asked, my earnest hopes for the Dumb One trumping my customary vigilance against Fray Luis's rhetorical trickeries.

'Ah! Trade secret, I'm afraid, dear comrade,' he said, patting my arm. 'But keep coming to the hearings. It will be a good show, I guarantee it.'

'Are you turning his soul? Are you getting him to repent?' I asked, suddenly furious, as if knowing I was being tricked but helpless to prevent it.

'Now there. Show me a little patience. Your boy will be out gorging on ham hocks quicker than Cortes turns in his grave.'

The *braggadocio* of the man. Sometimes I imagine it's but a game of his to say things that will get to me.

14 April

Let Fray Luis go on with his brags. In the meantime it is the Dumb One who will suffer.

Fray Sebastian has announced that he will most likely conclude his interrogatories tomorrow, the day after at the latest. As matters progress, with the Dumb One supplying nothing that helps his case, I cannot imagine any next step other than to order him to the torture. Fray Sebastian, with expressed regret or otherwise, will recommend it. The Inquisitor General and his colleagues, with expressed regret or otherwise, will order it.

17 April

I awoke this morning startled by the fear that perhaps the Dumb One has never understood how easy the path might be for him if he only confessed and repented. I racked my brain to see if I'd ever precisely explained to him how the process of reconciliation, in a case such as his, of an earnest and even heroic sort who might count on the full support of an officer of the Holy Office such as myself, would likely go for him. I could not remember ever doing so. Then I considered if Fray Luis would ever have bothered with such a representation. Surely not.

Therefore I went to the Dumb One today with the best of intentions, holding out the carrot, so to speak. He greeted me, I imagined, a bit sullenly. Fray Sebastian's interrogations of him concluded yesterday, and as of today he has nothing to do but stare at the walls.

Actually, I wonder what he does do with his time here alone. I do not imagine he prays, yet I often catch him, on my arrival, engaged in what seems to be some effort at thought or concentration. His own sin of pride, perhaps, to imagine he can think his way through to life's solution.

'Have they announced to you the day of your next appearance?' I asked.

He nodded yes.

'Has Fray Luis thoroughly explained to you the harsh measures that might be ordered against your physical being?'

He nodded yes again.

'Let me talk to you a moment about a happier alternative,' I said. 'Our Church is merciful, our Holy Office is merciful, you do know that, don't you?'

His nod to this last I sensed as more hesitant, but choosing to ignore any lack of conviction, I continued, 'So, for instance, if you confessed your heresy, and your regret for it, and begged pardon, I can very nearly assure you that not only would pardon be forthcoming, but that few if any punishments would be heaped on you as a result. I say this, in the event that fear of punishment is sealing your lips and preventing your reconciliation to the bosom of God. Surely you have heard, have you not, of the fate of some penitents, who have been imprisoned or suffered humiliations or had their worldly goods confiscated, in order that they be helped to make their slate clean with God. But your slate, so to speak, is already quite clean, and I am here to vouch for it. You will be treated lightly, sir, I can assure you... if you but open your heart.'

I believe I then heard the Dumb One's wordless voice say to my mind, 'And confess what isn't so?'

I repeated these words one by one back to the Dumb One. 'Is this what you say, is this what you think, that I am asking you to confess what isn't so?'

He regarded me soberly. He did not flinch. His nod became unnecessary.

May the Lord forgive my anger and turn it towards righteousness. 'Then either I, we, our Holy Office, are utterly blind, or it is you who must be made to see!' I shouted. 'There is no third choice, there is no more room to talk, back and forth, you and I, accusation, suggestion, denial, endless parrying, declarations of respect, all nothing, nothing, nothing! Do you know what awaits you? Let me be quite specific. Because it is not punishment we seek, but truth. You are not to be punished, you are to be given a last chance, do you hear me, son?

'Listen well. You will be brought to a room below and stripped of your clothes until you shiver in cold and shame. And in the beginning you will be hung and stretched. A rope, having been attached to your hands, will then be run through pulleys so that you may be raised to the torture chamber's heights, whereupon weights will be placed on your feet, and the rope let go with jerks and stops as if you were a puppet or a rag doll on a string, your feet never quite touching the floor, so that all the bones in your body are stretched most painfully one from the other. If the *garrucha* fails, then the bottles of water shall not. You will be tied to a trestle laced with rungs, the most painful of beds to lie in, and here a wet linen will be placed on your nose and mouth so that water from the first bottle may be poured through it in steady drips until you feel death's nearness by drowning. And that will be one bottle of water only, but then there will be a second bottle, a third, a fourth, and the garrotes that are in the sides of the trestle will be at the same time tightened against your sides until your stomach, already filled with the water, near explodes. And if the water is insufficient, there will be the fire. First your feet shall be oiled, then the flames brought to their most tender soles, and this, it has been said, in the most grievous pain of all, to which men prefer death. Do you have a livelier sense now of what faces you?'

The Dumb One, as throughout my tirade, maintained his sober expression, his eyes frozen on me.

'Then for mercy's sake, repent!' I fixed on him that fire-eyed gaze, my eyebrows bunched in accusation, which had served me well in several other cases over the years. One may call it play-acting, of course, but playing for the highest stakes.

Unfortunately, in the Dumb One's case, it had none of the desired effects. On the contrary, he laughed at me! Dear God, it was a laugh without a sound! His body crumpled, his face shook, his eyes twinkled, his lips spread happily to reveal a forest of crooked teeth, and yet not a sound!

'You mock me!' I declared.

And the Dumb One's voice returned to my mind. 'Because you look funny that way. Your eyes look like they are popping out of your head.'

I looked to the Dumb One for confirmation. All cheerfulness was gone from his expression.

'And because I can think of no other thing to do,' the voice continued. 'Because I am helpless.'

I said aloud to the Dumb One, so that there could be no possible mistake: 'On your own, yes, you are helpless. It is even the beginning of wisdom that you recognize it. But God can give you strength.'

'Nothing will happen by force,' the voice said.

'We shall see,' I said sadly.

Today being Friday, I had an instinct to check up on him later in the day. I arrived at his cell a little while before sunset. In a corner of the cell I could see a small candle lit, its wax melting into the dirt of the floor. One might presume that I would be astonished, but actually I was not, having become inured to the Dumb One's incorrigibility, or persistence, or whatever it should be called. He turned to face me with a look I cannot describe. Perhaps it was only the darkness or the candle's faint flicker that made his look so inscrutable. One moment I thought I saw in him pleading, and the next moment, compassion. The Dumb One having compassion for me? No words passed between us. I then left him, neither taking his candle nor so much as gesturing to him in any fashion.

I did, however, have a lively discussion with his jailer, about refusing the Dumb One any sort of illumination on Friday evenings, and being otherwise careful with his liberties. The Dumb One seemed to have prevailed upon the jailer for a modest candle before sunset. But now the jailer understands my requirements, and in return for his future compliance I promised not to take the matter up with Fray Jorge.

18 April

Today the torture was ordered. Fray Sebastian made a brief statement of advocacy, Fray Luis made an even more perfunctory statement in opposition, the three judges briefly conferred, and the Inquisitor General issued their joint decree. The only reason the matter did not proceed to the chamber today was the unavailability of Dr. Contrerez. It was said he was attending to an urgent appendicitis at the Royal Indian Hospital but expected to be present tomorrow.

Before ordering the torture, the Inquisitor General asked Fray Luis to attempt to determine if his client had anything finally to contribute, which might eliminate the necessity for the order. Fray Luis was then seen to be whispering into the Dumb One's ear. The Dumb One was then seen to shake his head emphatically after which Fray Luis announced to the court: 'The accused wishes the Tribunal to know that he is not what you think.'

I felt certain the Inquisitor General or another of the judges would take Fray Luis's bait, so to speak, and inquire, if he was not what they thought, then what was he? But none did so. The torture was ordered, then he was led out without another question asked. Provided the troubling appendix has been removed and our physician is available, tomorrow the Dumb One will encounter, whether he cares for it or not, his last, best chance for salvation. On one point the Dumb One and I agree. Man is a creature endowed with free will. But what will this pitiful wretch make of it?

18 April
later

More troubled thoughts. I shall be only an observer at the torture. I shall not have executive authority. But what if those in charge do not have a sincere care about the Dumb One's eternal salvation? What puts this again in my mind is the brevity of the exchange between the judges and the accused today. The I.G. asks if he has anything exculpatory to contribute, Fray Luis says 'My client wishes the Tribunal to know that he is not what you think,' and then, no follow-up questions from the judges! Were they asleep? A more cynical view now intrudes on my own sleep. They ask no follow-up questions because they don't want the Dumb One to be saved! They would almost rather he burn at the stake and in Hell, because in doing so, he would make a more striking example for others. After all, there has not been a relaxation in more than a year. One might not wish to have the larger community believe the Holy Office has gone suddenly lax. A little toughening-up might be thought in order. All these thoughts of course cross my mind as well. But they mustn't be acted upon at the expense of such justice and mercy as we may provide a living soul. The Dumb One is a hard case. Hard means may be necessary to bring him into the light. I fear there may be little resolve to make it happen.

Dear God, I pray continuously for any scrap of wisdom Your grace may spare my darkened mind. Do I accuse my colleagues falsely? Do I ask too much of the Dumb One? Banish cruelty from my soul, so that I may do Your will on earth.

(And, I wonder further, what has happened to Fray Luis's brags about establishing the Dumb One's innocence altogether? He has been remarkably quiet, for a man with a 'secret weapon'.)

20 April

The physician, Dr. Contrerez, did indeed appear today.

I was admitted to the chamber at exactly a quarter before ten this morning. It has undergone a bit of a refurbishment. The judges now sit on a moderately elevated platform, so that no part of the rigors imposed nor of the subject's responses shall escape them. It remains, nonetheless, a dank and rather cloistered dungeon, barely adequate to handle one subject at a time. I remember with vivid terror how, preparatory to the great *Auto* of last year, I was obliged to be present one day for the torture of seven judaizers at once, whose screams toppled over one another in such an incessant, horrid cacophony that if one of them had spontaneously confessed, we could scarcely have heard their words. My chair this morning was to one side of the judges, next to the recording secretary and across from Fray Sebastian. I had not seen either of the technicians of the torture, Xavier and Ramon – both, I should say, highly competent and professional men – since before my trip to the north. We exchanged pleasantries. Promptly, at the tenth hour, the Dumb One was brought in. I believe I saw a flickering of fear on his face. He held his head down to one side a bit stiffly and his mouth seemed tightly set. Though I do not know truly what would be the signs of fear in him, never having previously seen him afraid.

He was asked to strip off his clothes and he did so and this too was a revelation. The thinness of the man! Of course it was possible he'd eaten so little in the dungeon that he was now reduced to this; but I'd never seen man nor woman, even in these same circumstances, so slight. One's fingers could walk across his ribs, so to speak. His body also bore numerous scars and injuries, as if the results of a rigorous life.

And then, when he turned so that I could see him more frontally, an even greater surprise. He appeared to be circumcised! Or rather, some sort of butchery had been attempted of his foreskin, and there was a darkness and a scarring. I could not quite see the results precisely, but it certainly appeared, in intention at least, to be a circumcision. He was no longer as I had once observed him.

I wished to make my observation known to the Inquisitor General, but he was already embarked on his formalities, stating the object of the day's inquiry, the participants and procedures. If I could say one thing for our Inquisitor General, he knows his formalities. And I could imagine, with the *Suprema's* emissary on his way, he would particularly wish to avoid proceeding with inadequate or incomplete records. He again asked the Dumb One if he had anything to contribute on his own behalf, so that the day's proceedings might become unnecessary, and Fray Luis then conferred with the Dumb One and said once again, 'The accused wishes the Tribunal to know that he is not what you think.' The judges then looked to each other, with a skepticism approaching, in Fray Manuel's case, faint amusement, and asked nothing further. Nor did the judges seem to take note of the altered condition of the Dumb One's private aspects. (Then again, why would they, never having seen them previously and with other injuries to the Dumb One's body commanding equal attention?)

The proceedings then began in earnest. As I had predicted to the Dumb One, it began with the *garrucha*. I do not believe any Inquisitor does his job properly who does not feel a part of the pain that the subject feels. It is our duty to Christ, after all. And so it was that when they bound the Dumb One's hands behind him I felt the cutting of the cords on his wrists, and when they jerked him up I felt his body pull apart from itself and its profound desire but to fall, and when they let him go and jerked him up again I felt the grinding of his bones and the tearing of his ligaments. Father, I endeavor not to exaggerate this. Only an arrogant stupidity could cause one not in bodily pain himself to imagine that he feels fully the pain of another. Yet I did feel something.

The look on the Dumb One's face, as he was dropped and jerked up short, was of a kind of vast surprise. He did not show so much the hurt of his body as the hurt he felt that someone would impose such pain upon him. Some men under the torture appear wrathful and their eyes burn with the hope of revenge; the Dumb One, if I even dared imagine it, felt something else entirely, something more like simple sorrow. Of course, my personal feelings for the man and my knowledge of him may have influenced what I felt of his pain and saw of his emotion. Throughout the jerking, the Inquisitor General confined himself to asking the first of the three simple questions that define the entire case: did the Simpleton admit that his lighting of a candle on the Jewish sabbath amounted to heresy? The Inquisitor General asked the question after each jerk of the *garrucha*. To each putting of the question, the Dumb One at first made no response at all, almost as if he hadn't heard a thing, as if all his attention were turned inward. Then a small, uncertain shake of his head. I have heard of subjects so masterful at the black arts of witchcraft that they have learned how to avoid altogether the pains intended to be inflicted on their bodies. They bleed, their bones break, but they feel nothing. But I do not believe this was the case with the Dumb One, who winced and flinched and screwed up his face with every jerk of the rope. I believe he was simply being his stubborn, or stalwart, or impossible, self. He did not cry out once throughout the *garrucha*, which the Inquisitor General ordered stopped after exactly one half hour.

Dr. Contrerez then did his examination of the Dumb One, and declared that he was not in imminent danger of death.

One half hour is neither a particularly slight nor particularly excessive amount of time for the *garrucha*, depending, of course, on the subject's attitude and physical constitution, and on what is planned for the next steps. And so I had no quarrel with the Inquisitor General's decision to stop it when he did. It was only when he ordered the water torture, or more accurately, when the water torture was completed, that the gravest doubts and deepest fears entered my mind. I pray I am no lover of the torture. I pray I derive no pleasure from seeing even the wicked put to pain. But it must be seen in its proper balance. There is no question, it is a matter of record, that any number of souls have been led to confession and repentance through the imposition of reminders of their physical frailty. Surely among those souls were some whose repentances were false and hypocritical, and of these, some we have found out and some we haven't. But there have been manifestly, as well, even more souls who do not relapse to heresy, who continue to adhere to the truth and thus find their eternal reward. This is precisely the balance that must be ever before our minds: is it better to spare the body its rigors and suffer the soul to eternal damnation, or to impose all that the body can bear in the hope – and it is only a hope – that a soul, a precious soul, will be saved? If there were, perchance, a ninety-nine percent chance of salvation, would the imposition of the torture be worthwhile? What if there were but a fifty percent chance? What if there were a one percent chance, or a chance of one in a million? I say, even if it were one in a million. In the balance of God, is not one eternal life worth more than a million earthly ones, is it not worth more than all the lives yet lived on earth?

And all these calculations do not even begin to address the social dimension of heresy: where one has lost faith, is his heresy not a threat to the faith of others? Of course it is! We have only to see the results of Luther to see such a catastrophe written on the largest historical scale! Thus, one imposition of rigor, however painful even to those who administer it, may save not one but *millions* of souls.

I feel I may have digressed from my point, but only to make a larger one. I love this man I met in the desert. I love his soul, which is in gravest danger. I do not relish seeing his body put to pain, indeed I feel that pain in my bones. But what troubles me more, or rather, troubled me more, when the Inquisitor General halted the trial of water after two bottles only, was how, if this torture was to be the Dumb One's last, best chance for salvation, he was being short-changed on that chance. The linen sucked into his throat caused him to gag and struggle for breath and feel death's nearness even on the first bottle of water. By the second bottle, the garrotes made his stomach bulge to bursting. And what did the Inquisitor General do, after he asked the question again and the Dumb One defied him with a simple head shake? He simply stopped the torture. He ordered no more bottles of water. Instead, he again brought forth Dr. Contrerez.

I knew then with a fair certainty what was behind this. It was precisely what had kept me sleepless for nights. The Inquisitor General does not truly care what happens to the Dumb One's soul! He does not care enough to use every means to save it. Rather, he is content, after a modicum of effort, to allow the Dumb One to go his own way to the stake, and to eternal damnation, while being a convenient warning to others that our Holy Office is still to be feared! Sacrificing one soul so that, in theory anyway, others might be heedful and remain in grace!

And I can see the logic, unfortunately. Perhaps, if I did not care so much for this emaciated, naked madman in front of me, if he had not once saved my life, if he did not possess kindness and courage that I had seen, I might even go along with it.

But instead, I confess, dear God, I wanted the I.G. to pile on the torture! Four bottles of water, six bottles, whatever it took, until the Dumb One's stubborn, self-defeating will would be broken, Satan's grip on him relaxed, and Your holy grace triumphant. So great was my anxiety that I wished to rush to the Inquisitor General and whisper in his ear: *Don't stop! Heap it on!*

What stopped me? Possibly it was my sense of propriety, as I was of course keenly aware of the inappropriateness of a mere witness, present at a proceeding only by the grace of its presiding officers, interfering and suggesting a course of conduct to the very judges who had invited him. Or perhaps it was my fear of angering the Inquisitor General when the *Suprema's* emissary is expected at any moment and my chances of a transfer may hang on his enthused recommendation. Or perhaps it was because I am a liar and hypocrite to the core and all my fine proclamations of principle amount to nothing and I could not bear any further the Dumb One's earthly pain.

The third portion of the torture, the fire, proceeded as the others, with unimpeachable correctness of form and utter lack of passion. Oil on his feet, flame on his feet, finally his screams of agony, the question, the terse answer, the flame again, the question again, ten minutes, the flame, the question, then a halt. Torture by the book. Nothing more, nothing less. And no

results. Unless the result, that the Dumb One remained unconfessed, that he thus becomes the perfect candidate for the stake,
was all that was ever really intended.

THE TRIAL

entries of 23 April 1650

23 April

I shall try to record the day's events with as much objectivity and absence of emotional coloration as I can bring to developments that even now as I write make me tremble when I hold my pen.

Today was the fourth day following the Dumb One's torture and he was deemed well enough to appear once again before the Tribunal.

Today was also to be the day scheduled for Fray Luis to present evidence on the Dumb One's behalf.

The Dumb One was led in promptly and taken to the witness chair. I could not observe on him any marks of physical injury, however he walked delicately and was assisted, so that I presumed his feet continued to be inflamed. In distinction to the day of his torture, this morning he shot me a glance as he entered. I could read little into it and nodded tightly in response. I have not visited him in his jail for several days. It is not for lack of interest, but I felt I could not reward his obstinacy, and at the same time did not wish to berate him for it when he was already suffering grievous wounds.

Fray Luis entered with his customary flourish. He seems constitutionally incapable of letting his clothing simply hang from him. Whatever room he enters, it is always in a swirl of robes. How pathetic. How utterly annoying. These were my reactions.

The Inquisitor General asked Fray Luis how he cared to proceed and Fray Luis stood and pronounced as follows: 'It will be a simple defense, your honor. I have only a single question to put to the subject.'

'Proceed, then,' the Inquisitor General ordered.

'Of course, sir,' Fray Luis said.

I trembled for what I felt was certain to be the vast inadequacy of his defense. Fray Luis showing himself a member of the team, an exemplary vessel of the Holy Office, at the Dumb One's expense – I suppose that is what I thought, when I heard the phrase 'a single question'. I brimmed with indignation.

But I was to be as disappointed in my indignation as I was by the subsequent outcome.

Fray Luis stood before the Dumb One and pursed his lips as though deciding how he should phrase his fateful question. Perhaps he was even intending the effect of a magician, about to pull something from his hat. If he had right then winked, at the Inquisitor General, at the Dumb One, even at myself, I would not have been entirely surprised.

Then he said to the Dumb One: 'Please inform the Holy Office. Have you ever been baptized?'

With absolute clarity, the Dumb One shook his head in rhythmic turns, left then right then left, like the pendulum of a clock. His face was a mask. To make this awful denial, he had turned himself into a machine.

Fray Luis pivoted to address the panel of judges. From that moment forward I don't believe that he glanced even once at his client. It was as if the Dumb One no longer existed for him, as if nothing that happened next even concerned the Dumb One. He addressed the judges as follows (I shall reconstruct as best I am able): 'We have here today, your honors, I should not say a miscarriage of justice, but a miscarriage of jurisdiction, an offense against ourselves, so to speak. I say it is no miscarriage of justice because truly this vile, contemptible, filthy, faithless individual that sits before you deserves anything wretched that life might deal him. He is not to be trusted, admired or loved for what he is today. What you see before you is a calamity of a man, a sorry excuse of a man, a parody of a man, whose lack of words is indeed the mark of an equal absence of spirit. No, it is no injustice that was meted out to him by the *garrucha* and the fire or even by his incarceration. He deserves it all! And yet he also deserves nothing! Why is this? How can this be?

'Because, your honors: he is not one of us. By his own testimony, uncontraverted, he is unbaptized. Indeed, what you have before you, dear judges and colleagues, is not a Christian heretic, not a *converso* or *Marrano,* who tried out Christianity for convenience's sake, found it not to his liking and relapsed; no, what you have here is far, far worse. What you have before you is a not a judaizer, but a Jew!

'So much a Jew is this man that when I uncovered to him that he was not circumcised, he took it upon himself, in the very cell where we incarcerated him, to do the botched job upon himself! Those that might say, well, surely, he circumcised himself only in order to evade the stake, such people do not stop to think that no one would do such an act in the hopes of being believed. For, of course, it is incredible. Only an idiot would think he could persuade our Holy Office with such crudity, and the Jew, my dear colleagues, may be a madman, but he is never an idiot! And he may have a cunning heart, but he indicated the exact same truth on the day of his torture when you asked him if his lighting a candle on the Jewish sabbath amounted to heresy and he answered each time with silent negation. Because how can a Jew commit Christian heresy?

'Our sanctified Church and Hispanic Majesties established our Holy Office to deal with the errors of Christians, not with the superstitions and repulsive customs of a man such as this. God shall take care of the Jews, shall prepare for them their just desserts. We must take care of our flock. The formula is simple. No baptism, no jurisdiction. Therefore I pray you, no, I demand of you, not for his wretched sake, but for our own, for our mission's purity and truth, that you dismiss this case at once.'

Fray Luis concluded and retook his chair without yet noticing his client. The Dumb One had sat impassively, as if uncomprehending, through it all.

The Inquisitor General called for a recess, so that he might confer with his colleagues. The judges appeared perturbed, their brows were furrowed and there was already whispering among them.

I confess that at this moment I was overcome with the most intense and absurd contradictions of feeling. If I could so put it, I felt Satan place all his weight upon me. On the one hand, if I now did nothing, it was apparent the Dumb One might presently walk out of the Tribunal hall a free man. I even felt a delight in this possibility. He could go back to that girl of Nuevo Leon, whom he never spent a night without a dream of, he could live such a 'free' life as he pleased, he could believe as he wished, have children as he wished, enjoy the bounties of the earth in proportion as he earned them. Dear God, I was not blind to the world's possibilities; on the contrary, in those few moments, I lived them all, in another man's fate. But Your infinite wisdom did not desert me. I knew in the depths of my heart that his days would soon be over, illness and suffering would overtake him, and what comfort would there be for him then? Nothing. Only eternal nightmare, that begins even on this earth, when one sees what must be coming.

Yet even then I felt there could be a sort of justice in seeing the Dumb One walk free. If it were true that he was a Jew, then what right had I to interdict his inherent free will, what right had I, finally, to save a soul that would not choose to be saved? I might try, but indeed I had tried, and manifestly failed. The sticking point, finally, was not the Dumb One, but myself. I, after all, knew what the judges did not know: that Fray Luis's entire case, the very heart and premise of it, was a lie.

I prayed for understanding, I prayed for calm to enter my soul.

Then I found Fray Luis in the courtyard, standing alone, breathing in the spring air. 'Nicely argued,' I said upon my approach.

'I may have made a bit of a mockery of you,' he said. 'Sorry about that, but you must admit, you rather deserved it. And I didn't mention you by name. I didn't say, "Why has Fray Alonso wasted our time with this pitiful case?"'

'I found no mockery,' I said.

'Oh? Then perhaps you weren't listening between the lines.'

'You did not say, for instance, "Why did Fray Alonso not even bother to check his prisoner's baptism?"'

'No I did not.'

'And the reason you did not? Let me guess. It was certainly not because you knew I *had* checked the Dumb One's baptism. No, it wouldn't be that, because you would not know that I had, would you?'

I stalked away from him, in the manner of an advocate who does not want his witness to get in the last word.

But a certain curiosity got the better of me. I halted my steps. 'Why was it, Fray Luis, pray explain, if you were so confident of your case, that you did not put it forth previously and save your client the torture?'

'You are joking, aren't you? The torture could only add to his credibility. And besides, why shouldn't a Jew suffer?'

My Lord and Savior, have I sufficiently indicated how repugnant I find Your supposed servant Fray Luis?

I went directly to Fray Sebastian and made arrangements for him to call me to testify.

When the Tribunal was called back into session, I was the first witness to be called. When I saw the Dumb One in his box, I felt the agony of Judas, competing in me with the sword of righteousness. *I must betray you to be true to myself. I serve you by betraying you. I serve God by betraying you.* These were my thoughts, dear Lord. For, despite every duty that truth imposed on me, I did not want to see the Dumb One perish. He gave me one questioning look. What was he questioning?

Fray Sebastian asked me, 'Is there a means by which this Tribunal can establish whether the subject be Jew or Christian?'

'There is,' I said. 'A leather pouch hangs from his neck. Examine its contents, for it contains his certificate of baptism.'

The Inspector General then ordered that the leather pouch, hidden as usual from view by the Dumb One's tunic, be discovered and examined.

The Dumb One's neck appeared to freeze, as Fray Sebastian opened his tunic to reveal the small pouch and proceeded to lift it over his head. The Dumb One's eyes were full of fright. I thought he would try to snatch the pouch back, but he did not.

Fray Sebastian questioned me: 'Is this the leather pouch you referred to?'

'It is,' I said.

'I will open it myself,' the Inquisitor General said.

And so Fray Sebastian brought it to him. The Inquisitor General loosened its strings, inserted his fingers into the sack, and brought forth a folded sheet of paper.

He unfolded it, examined it, then pronounced: 'There is nothing on this sheet of paper. It is empty. It is a blank.' He showed the blank paper up to the entire court.

I believe I was no more shocked than I had been at Fray Luis's initial lie. If he would stoop to calling the Dumb One a Jew, would he not stoop to removing the proof that it was not so? Nonetheless, the Tribunal hall hummed with the murmurs of surprise. Fray Luis had played another trump. This time I truly did feel as though I'd been made the fool, and not least by my own doing.

I confess the rage I felt. Only then did I notice the Dumb One regarding me. Again it was with that look of curiosity, as if he wondered truly what I was doing, or why.

Fray Sebastian requested a recess, which was granted. With grave embarrassment, but no less determination, I went to him. By then I had wracked my brain to think if I could possibly have been mistaken, or dreamed the certificate when there wasn't one, or suffered some mental lapse or hallucination. Could Satan, even, have confused my mind, so that I would cause endless troubles to this innocent whom I cared for? Of course not, of course not. I had seen the baptismal certificate, seen its Latin letters, felt its crisp folds. 'Let me testify further,' I said to Fray Sebastian. 'I can testify that I saw this certificate myself, read it with my own eyes, and surely I will be believed over this Dumb

One. It is obvious, to further his case, that the certificate was simply removed and a blank piece of paper, a trap, set in its place.'

So Fray Sebastian, indulging me with a longstanding colleague's compassion, brought me back to witness once more.

'Tell us, Fray Alonso,' he said. 'Did there come a time when you first saw this leather pouch yourself?'

'Yes. When I was on the trail with the subject, from Santa Fe in the north to here.'

'Did there come a time when with your own eyes you saw the contents of that pouch?'

'Yes.'

'Tell us the circumstances.'

'The subject was asleep, drunk on wine. My desire to prove his judaizing intentions got the better of me, I opened the pouch expecting to find Hebrew letters or some such that might prove the subject's backsliding, but I found instead, to my disappointment at the time, his certificate of baptism, in Latin letters. I placed it back in the subject's pouch while he slept and said nothing to him about it.'

'And do you swear to the truth of these facts, to God and on your honor as an officer of the Tribunal of the Holy Office of the Supreme and General Inquisition in and for the Colony of New Spain?'

'I do.'

Fray Sebastian seated himself but, predictably enough, Fray Luis arose in a swirl of concern. 'May I question the witness?'

'You may,' said the Inquisitor General.

'Fray Alonso, how long have you been a functionary of the Holy Office?'

'Thirteen years.'

'And during those thirteen years, have you ever been asked to perform a duty you more detested, a duty you thought more an utter waste of time, a greater diversion of your talents, than that mission on which you were sent to seek out heretics in the northern regions? Really, you made no great secret of your feelings, did you?'

'No, I did not. And yes, I did feel I could be of better use elsewhere.'

'Did you perhaps feel, even, that being sent there was an indication that you were out of favor with your superiors?'

'I had such thoughts from time to time.'

'And when you were in Nuevo Leon, did you uncover any heresy or did you fail to?'

'I failed to.'

'And when you were in Santa Fe, did you uncover heresy or did you fail to?'

'I failed to.'

'It is true, is it not, that for all your journeying of very nearly a year, the only supposed "heresy" you uncovered was the supposed heresy of the subject before us today?'

'That is correct. Which I must say tends to prove my initial assumption.'

'Yes, indeed. Thank you, Fray Alonso.'

Fray Luis turned to address the panel of judges.

'I put it to you, my colleagues. We have heard that Fray Alonso feared he was in disfavor and despised his mission and came up with only one suspect after a year's trolling at the Holy Office's considerable expense. If his one pitiful suspect were on the verge of walking free, would he not have a powerful motive to lie in order to prevent that? What a fool he might seem, to himself and others, what a blow it would be to his future chances of promotion, if his one miserable candidate for the *quemadero* be shown to be not a candidate at all!'

'I resent your inferences! I resent your corruption!' I shouted.

Fray Luis ignored me and continued with the judges. 'Fray Alonso may resent as much as he wants, but it is a question now simply of who is to be believed, Fray Alonso who says the subject was baptized, and the subject himself who says he was not. And I put it further to the court. The one has a powerful motive to lie, whereas the other, the subject before us… who in all the realms of Christendom would allow himself to be called a Jew if he were not?'

'Allow me, your honors, allow me!' I stood up and shouted again. 'I have proof! I have final proof! Allow me!' For I had sworn that Fray Luis, no matter what, would no longer get the best of me. May God deal with me justly and mercifully, but in my rage I scarcely thought of the Dumb One. I simply wanted to prove the absurdity of Fray Luis and all his infinite condescension.

I was out of order, of course. Yet the Inquisitor General,

sensing anyway the sincerity of my passion, indulged me some-what. He called another recess. I conferred with Fray Sebastian and within an hour returned to the court, bearing with me, yes, this very journal I am inscribing just now.

This journal. This dear journal, which speaks the truth when others cannot.

I had marked those pages which specifically proved what I knew must be proved. I was aware that if the judges strayed too far from these, to certain of the pages where I wrote of the Dumb One's 'voice', they might think me rather mad. At the minimum, under Fray Luis's grueling tutelage, I would have much explaining to do, about my private connection to You. But I guessed that our judges' lazy eyes would not stray too far. And in all events it was too late. My integrity, all that I had ever stood for as an inquisitor, was already in shreds. 'I have final proof!' I had shouted.

I took the witness chair. The Dumb One watched with, now, what I imagined, was bated breath. He sat with a perfect still-ness. One could not detect even if air was going in or out. Fray Sebastian asked me, 'What is it that you have in your hand, Fray Alonso?'

'A journal,' I said. 'A journal which you kindly gifted me with more than a year ago when you returned from Seville.'

'And have you written in this journal every night?'

'Not every night, but many.'

'And did there come nights when you had occasion to record your observations concerning the subject's leather pouch and his baptism?'

'There were such nights.'

'And was it your practice, when you did record matters such as the subject's leather pouch and his baptism, to record them promptly, so that your memory might not falter?'

'It was.'

'You never waited, say, three months, or even one month, to make a record?'

'I did not. I have treated this journal as a confessional, and made records accordingly.'

'Would you show the Tribunal, Fray Alonso, those very pages which recorded your investigations as to the contents of the subject's leather pouch and as to his baptism?'

'Yes, of course.'

And so I did. I handed them this very journal, opened to those 'relevant' pages that I had earmarked. I betrayed, as best I was able, no anxiety that their eyes might stray further.

The Inquisitor General and the other judges considered my pages with the greatest interest, reading here and there, pointing out key sentences to one another, making observations as to the entirety, and completeness, of my record. I watched their fingers, I watched their eyes, praying that curiosity not lead them too far afield.

Meanwhile Fray Sebastian, who had shown me such admirable indulgence whilst I flailed around earlier, concluded his presentation with the following encomium which caused even my ears to burn with embarrassment: 'You will see that Fray Alonso's journal is comprehensive and detailed. And it contains every confirmation that Fray Alonso observed exactly what he said he observed and learned what he learned. For if the diary were not true, it would all have to be a monstrous lie, a gigantic fiction, perpetrated by its author over many months and for no motive that can be discerned. If you disbelieve this journal, you would have to credit Fray Alonso with being some mad or evil genius, to invent so much for so little reason. Surely he could not have anticipated the use to which it is being put today. What you see before you is an officer of this Tribunal acting with the greatest scruples. We must not mock him. We must believe him.'

Even as Fray Sebastian concluded his plea, the judges continued to peruse these pages of mine. But their attentions remained on the earmarked pages. Whatever my embarrassment at Fray Sebastian's praises, when the Inquisitor General closed my book in front of him, I knew that I had won.

The Dumb One was led away. I wish I could report he gave me a parting glance, but he did not. I have not a single idea what he thought. Fray Luis declined to ask me questions. He could see that the day was done.

Or perhaps he was afraid more for himself than for his client, perhaps he feared that if he questioned me directly I would somehow turn the tables on him, and, with integrity now in my court, show him for the liar and manipulator that he was. Indeed, I might have done just that. I was itching to try.

And yet, tonight, I realize, Fray Luis comes out of all this quite unscathed. His client will be condemned after all, which is apparently what everyone wants. He will have shown himself to be a vigorous advocate, without actually upending any boats.

As for myself, I am utterly exhausted. I do not even know if I am more sinned against or sinning. I take no pleasure in the Dumb One's defeat. But why did he lie?

23 April
later

I have just received a note, slipped under my door while I was writing the foregoing.

I read with shaking hands:

Does it not take one marrano to know another?

AS A WITHERED BRANCH

entries from 24 April 1650 to 1 May 1650

Incessant, unwanted speculations concerning the anonymous note that I have received. Who sent it? Why? What does it mean? What ought I to do about it?

The meaning, I have concluded, is unmistakable. I am accused of being a *Marrano*, a converted secret Jew. Or in all events of having *Marrano* blood in my veins. Not that I imagine the author of such a note would for one instant acknowledge the distinction.

My Lord and Savior Jesus Christ, I acknowledge the crosses I must bear. But the insult of this dank, airless lie is so great that I fear without Your intervention I will fail to withstand it with Christian courage, Christian grace.

To begin, of course, the perpetrator might be anyone with nightly access to our Inquisitorial residences. This should properly include the entire city's population, since anyone could in logic pass a note by means of an unwitting resident. But then the resident, if unwitting, might readily confess and be uncovered, and hence the perpetrator. Thus I conclude that the sender is one of us, a witting resident of the Holy Office dormitories. Seventy-six persons reside here. But the note said 'Does it not take one *Marrano* to know another?' This implies a reference to the case against the Dumb One, in which I of course identified him as of *Marrano* extraction. These proceedings being held in guarded secrecy, it remains possible to imagine some violation of that secrecy, but in all probability, so logic and intuition both tell me, the perpetrator is from among those who had access to the Dumb One's trial. The judges, the lawyers, the recorder, the administrators of the torture, Dr. Contrerez, the officers of security. Of these, none to my knowledge has expressed antipathy towards me, or suspicion of me. Indeed, I do not feel I compliment myself excessively to say that they regard me as one of the 'old guard', even, as is said, the 'office historian', the man who knows where the bones are buried. With one exception. One exception who regards me with condescension, pity, contempt. Fray Luis.

I reach this conclusion logically on paper, but in fact my soul is in utter uproar, I scream inside, Fray Luis! Fray Luis! Fray Luis!

Who else? And what does he know, what has he done, what does he plan?

I know that I am no *Marrano* myself, I have of course a comprehensive knowledge of Jewish practices and adhere to none of them, but how can I be sure of my ancestors? Has Fray Luis done a search? If so, it occurs to me precisely how he has done so! He has taken the testimony of my deposition in which I report my conversation with the Dumb One regarding ancestors – Don Tomas Rodrigues de Santangel whom the Dumb One claimed to be his own, and Don Federico de la Ronda, who was most certainly mine – and matched these names against the ancient archives of our own Holy Office concerning suspected *Marranos*. Did I myself not once voice the suspicion, did it not make its way even into my deposition, that the Dumb One's *Marrano* ancestor might have been the very conquistador to whom he claims descent with such pride? When Fray Luis looked up the Dumb One's ancestor, he troubled himself to research mine as well!

Yes, this is what he has done, if he has done anything at all except to conceive this torture to pay me back for my defeat of him in court!

But it is impossible! My mind tells me it is impossible, that Don Federico de la Ronda, the conquistador, my great ancestor, should have been a *Marrano*.

But why is it impossible? Of course it is possible! I have never checked. How should I know? Does my blood tell me? That is absurd!

I will go at once! I will examine the archives myself.

But no! Of course, this is precisely what Fray Luis wants me to do! He will be watching the archives like a hawk. He or his spies will see me entering. He will want to catch me out in my own guilt!

No, I will avoid the archives at all cost. Moreover, I will tell no one about this note. No one must know. Who can say what it might cost me? A transfer to Spain? More?

And perhaps, just perhaps, if I am silent myself, and Fray Luis spreads this vile rumor to others, I will be able once again to turn the tables on him, as I did in court, by showing that his scandal-mongering, sly, ignoble behavior is a far greater disgrace than a distant ancestor of mine!

Perhaps, only perhaps.

Heavenly Father, save me from the wicked intentions of my enemies, preserve me from disgrace!

The cruelest thought is that I am no longer certain who I am.

25 April

The Dumb One was condemned today. He will be relaxed to the secular authority. The *quemadero* will be prepared.

When he was asked, after the Inquisitor General's pronounce-ment, if he had anything to say on his own behalf, he indicated that he did not. As on previous occasions, Fray Luis excerpted something from my testimony and inquired of the Dumb One whether he cared to affirm it. Apparently he did. 'My client wishes the Tribunal to know that he lives his life as if there is God.'

'What God?' the Inquisitor General asked, showing at last one spark of curiosity.

Again, whispers, gestures, between Fray Luis and the Dumb One. 'A God of love,' Fray Luis said.

This exchange produced angry whispers in the tribunal hall. The harsh judgment of the whisperers was that the Dumb One, with his fateful 'as if', was tightly in Satan's grasp. This evening, I am not so sure. He scarcely noticed me today, or anyway he paid me no mind. I cannot begin to fathom what he thinks of me now. But I feel, as if it were an intimation, that when the Dumb One permitted to be uttered in his name the words, 'A God of love', it was not entirely from a position of unbelief. It was as if he were reaching out, as far as his arms could reach. To live one's life as if there is a God of love. I shall ponder this. How evil can that be? How far from Jesus Christ our Savior can a man who lives by such words be? I am not sure I have the answer. But I know that the others' harsh words for him, I know their lack of pity, do not begin to comprehend this situation that God Himself has surely put to us.

I remember him now, not as we now find him, emaciated and hollow-cheeked, crabbed by the application of the torture, but as he was when I first 'found him out', with his sabbath candle lit, by his cook fire in the desert. The sweep of his sandy hair, the sparks of the fire that glistened in the dark almonds of his eyes, the unlined face that was like a boy's face, the smell of cod-fish on his hands. Seldom have I had a stronger impression of a man who believed he was doing nothing wrong. I fear that that itself is now a sign of his damnation.

I should add that, despite my intense anticipation, Fray Luis paid me not a glance today in court. No look of condescension, no smirk, no knowingness. He was too busy making sure the Dumb One was thoroughly condemned.

26 April

The date for the Dumb One's relaxation has been set. The *quemadero* shall be ready by the thirtieth, and shall be lit on the first of May.

There is now, according to every precedent, little if any chance of him escaping death. Our current Inquisitor General has been firm in rejecting every exception. Even if he repents, the most the Dumb One might now expect is a change in the means of execution.

27 April

I am of the opinion today that the Dumb One may in truth wish to die. Fray Jorge informed me that when he was deprived of a candle two nights ago, he wailed bitterly and inconsolably. My diagnosis is that his devotion to whatever that candle represents to him is so great that he would rather perish than suffer the shame of neglecting it.

The more terrible shame is that he does not even seem to know what it represents. Something grips his mind, which he cannot see, or which we cannot see, or which cannot be seen.

In the meantime, I do not go to him. Each morning I awake and say that I will go. And then I do not, I find other necessary things, I plot out my time until there is none left and then I say I will go to him tomorrow. I have not spoken to him since I testified before the Tribunal and prevented his acquittal. Perhaps it is best that I not even try to say anything to him, or him to me. Recriminations would result, and recriminations are sinful. Ah yes, Fray Alonso, you are facile with excuses. You are simply afraid to go.

And why is that? Dear God, I pray it is not from fear that Fray Luis will use this much more against me, that, secret *Marrano* that I am, I have formed an affection for another of my kind. I search my soul. I do not find such fear. But I am a weak, fallen, useless man, who without Your guidance and grace could no more find the truth of my soul than a needle in a stack of hay.

29 April

This afternoon I did visit the Dumb One in his cell. I was conscious then, and am conscious now, that it may have been my last chance to speak with him. The preparations for the *Auto* are well advanced. The secular authorities are making their preparations, practicalities are being attended to, by tomorrow a mere interested party such as myself may well be considered to be getting in the way.

I entered with a grave countenance that, however appropriate it was to his circumstances, nonetheless felt false on my face. Why did I still imagine I could impress something on him?

He had an unsurprised expression, as if he knew I would be along sooner or later. He greeted me with a nod. He sat on his stool and did not get up. Even on his stool, he moved gingerly, as if the injuries of the torture might still abide internally. I sat down on the floor so as to be more at his height, and I said to him, 'There are many things we could talk about, but all are inconsequential save one. Are you ready now to confess the errors in your thinking and belief, and be accepted back into the bosom of your Holy Church, which is merciful to penitents? I cannot promise you an escape from imminent death, but I can promise you an easier one, where you will not be burned until once you are dead by strangulation. I apologize for my words' harshness, but it would be harsher still at this moment not to face realities. And the larger reality is infinitely greater. Repent now and you may still see Heaven!'

He stared at me with the sort of benign, questioning steadiness that I imagined might animate the expression of one hesitating between a blessing and a curse. His old look of curiosity, but now more intense, more focused, as if aware of how little time was left.

'I am sorry it was I who had to speak against you,' I finally said. 'But you lied when you said that you had not been baptized.'

'Because I was weak. Because I wished to see my wife. Fray Luis told me…' his 'voice' said wordlessly to my mind.

Then he wept, with great drama and lack of control, as Fray Jorge had reported him weeping when he was deprived of his Friday candle. He wept copiously and continuously, and averted his face from mine. With greatest embarrassment, as I believed, he then pushed his arms out in my direction, urging me to leave. Or did I only imagine that was his intention? Could it have been my own embarrassment, and not his, that drove me away? The most likely case of all is that it was the embarrassment of us both. Shame drove us apart.

I could not say words that would help him. We each, I'm sure, blamed the other and blamed ourselves.

I left him to the drama of his tears.

My own arrogance astonishes me. It is one thing to be

29 April
later

My previous entry was interrupted, mid-sentence, as I now observe many hours later, by a porter's knock. So thoroughly was I disturbed that I do not now recall how that last sentence was intended to end.

The porter informed me that there was someone outside the dormitory's gates with my name and an urgent wish to see me.

My first reaction was to believe the visitor had something to do with the note I had received. Would I now have the chance to confront the scoundrel face-to-face? Had Fray Luis sent an agent? I asked the porter why he had not shown the individual in. He said that it would not be appropriate. I put down my pen, donned my cloak, and immediately went down with him.

Just outside the gates stood a small, huddled figure that appeared, in the cool of the evening, to be shivering. I could neither imagine nor discern who it was, and I felt a certain trepidation, as if I were approaching a ghost.

'Do you know me? Do you remember?' It was a small, uncultured, woman's voice, shy and pleading. As I came near her, she dropped her scarf and gripped my arm, and I surely knew her face. She smelled of having recently lived roughly. 'Fray Alonso, please, may you help me,' she pleaded, gripping my arm more tightly.

'What is it, Felicia?' I asked, but the poor thing could hardly get words out as her shivering grew more intense. 'How have you come here? Tell me. Have you come to see your friend?'

'Yes, of course, yes!' she cried, and struggled to hold her teeth from further chattering. 'Please, Fray Alonso, for two days I've come to the place where they hold him, and they'll not let me in because they say I'm nothing to him. I say I'm his wife. This they don't believe. I ask them, is it true, I see everywhere signs on the streets that he will be burned, and they laugh at me as though it's a stupid question. Can it be that he's to be burned and I can't even see him? Then I thought, would *you* take me? Surely if you told them, then I could see him.'

These were not her precise words, which were less coherent, with many hesitations and confusions, but her meaning was thus.

I had a deep desire to loosen her grip from my arm, and even to distance myself from her aromatic charms, but instead, or perhaps in the hope that she would then loosen her grip, I said, 'Yes, Felicia. Come with me. We'll see what we can do.'

But she did not loosen it, we walked off towards the prison together with her grip on me tighter than ever, such that my steps slowed with hers. There were moments when I felt as if I were being led home by a whore.

At the prison I roused the jailer whom I'd previously intimidated, and announced, 'This woman is in my care. I apologize for coming past the dinner hour. But may we see the condemned?'

On the way coming over I had asked her a few questions and from her answers discerned that she had longed for the Dumb One, that she was pregnant with his child, that she had left whatever she had in Monterrey to come to him, that she had most likely whored herself to a train of traders to make her passage from Monterrey to here (she did not say this explicitly – she had a certain modesty of expression – yet I felt it must be the case) and that she had had no idea of the grave situation of her beloved until she arrived here and began her search for him and saw signs on the streets announcing the Act of Faith respecting one 'Juan del Paso del Norte,' which one of the traders who gave her passage read aloud to her.

When the jailer announced to the Dumb One my arrival with

a 'woman visitor' he rushed to the bars with vast anticipation. I have never seen so happy a condemned man as when their faces met. The bars between them added only poignancy to their efforts to touch and hold each other. There were tears, abundant tears, as well.

Relying on my honor, the jailer let both of us into his cell. Relying on my honor, as well, he retreated to his station. It became apparent to me soon enough that I had nothing to say, nothing to add. I felt my time could be better spent allowing them their moments of peace. She fussed over him, worried for him, complained about his wan condition, expressed outrage and pity at all that had been done to him. I was taken aback, actually, by her words, simply because she had so many of them, something I had not suspected. I called for the jailer again. I had determined to give them one half hour alone together. The jailer led me back into the corridor. I told him I would remain in charge of the prisoner and would call for him again when needed. Alone now, I retreated to the stairway and began to estimate the passing time. I will confess that I did hear sighs and moans, but however they spent that one-half hour otherwise remains between themselves and their Maker. Dear God, punish me surely if You must for my sin of complicity, but I don't know that I could do otherwise even if given a second chance.

In due time I returned to face them through the bars. Even in the dimness of the dungeon light, I could tell that their minutes together had worked a kind of transformation, in their physical manifestations anyway. His cheeks were full as if he had never been tortured, his eyes glistened with a mortal happiness. Her native skin shone with that moonlit sheen which I remembered him once roughly approximating in the dirt. Her face was round and clean, lacking any line of concern, and her belly seemed to swell with pride, not shame. She had become, as it were, the exact person he once imagined.

And while the aromas of the trail still abode on her, I was certain he did not notice. Indeed, the dank odor of the dungeon clung to his own clothes and skin, and I'm sure, if they'd ever noticed, they would have competed with each other in rankness.

'Will you marry us?' Felicia said.

'But you told me you were already married,' I said.

'But you told him we were not,' she said.

Is a condemned man forbidden the sacrament of marriage? Is conviction of heresy a fatal bar to an act which would ameliorate a sin? It was not a question that I had ever faced, nor had I books with me to determine an answer, nor when I prayed for guidance did You guide me otherwise. Therefore, seeing no reason why I should not, I married them.

It was all done with low voices, so that the jailer would not hear.

I then allowed them a further hour together alone, at the conclusion of which I called for the jailer.

The Dumb One thanked me, if he thanked me at all, with a stare.

I made a last try by asking him, 'Have you anything to confess and repent of?'

He looked at me, I thought, as if he had truly heard my question for the first time. Then his 'voice' said something shocking in the mirroring of my thought. 'This will be the last time I speak. If I repent… could I escape my death?'

I felt an overwhelming urge to lie, to tell him, yes, your future on this earth is bright, you will go with your wife and your child to wherever it is you imagine and live a life blessed by God.

What harm could come of him saying, 'I repent,' even if he did so only because the girl was with him now?

But he had always been sincere with me. Sincere to a fault, sincere even to his death. Should I lie to him now?

'I don't believe your corporeal life can be saved,' I said. 'But as for your eternal life in a resurrected Christ…'

His eyes, his silence. He seemed to thank me for the truth.

I took Felicia out with me. I instructed the jailer that she was the prisoner's lawful wife and had been so, and that if it was possible during the next day to permit her further brief visits with her man, it should be done.

Now I am in my room, at a most extraordinarily late hour. The girl has found tavern quarters. I believe I have had my last conversation on earth with the Dumb One. The thought of his marriage, and the girl's serene young face, bring me to tears. God's will be done.

30 April

I know so little about mortal love between man and woman. I am persuaded it is not something one learns from books, and of course I have had little personal experience. Yet I seem to have found myself, somehow, to be such a love's facilitator. Much to ponder, much to confess.

30 April
afternoon

Today the emissary of the *Suprema* arrived. Actually, he arrived last evening, exhausted from an arduous and delayed journey, but this morning he made his first appearance among us. He is Diego Hernando Montalves, no more than thirty years old, slender, of quite striking and masculine an appearance, with abundant dark hair and brows, and a rather long, narrow face that concentrates the intensity of his gaze and suggests considerable discernment. He has already, at his tender age, served as head constable of the Holy Office in Valladolid. He is, by all accounts, a 'comer'.

I was hoping to be invited to lunch with him. Indeed I went immediately this morning to the Inquisitor General's office with that request. However, his secretary informed me that the I.G. was in a vital meeting, and it remained for me only to leave him a feeble message in writing. Nothing came of it.

Instead, I went to the refectory at noon, hoping anyway to intercept the emissary's party and casually introduce myself. I was not surprised to see the Inquisitor General leading the emissary and his party towards his private dining quarters. What did shock me, however, was to see who accompanied them as the Inquisitor General's apparent guest: Fray Luis.

I aborted my thought of approaching Diego Hernando Montalves. I realized that if I did so, it would readily provide Fray Luis the occasion, out of my hearing, to say the most disparaging things against me, even, perhaps, to use this earliest opportunity to divulge his poisonous 'secret'.

But failing to make the emissary's early acquaintance is the least of my concerns. What I deduce, in the starkest terms, is that Fray Luis has been lying in wait for the *Suprema's* representative all along. With startling clarity I now see the full extent of his plot. I made no secret last year of my desire for a transfer to Spain. At the time it was fully expected that the emissary's arrival was only months away. It must be that Fray Luis himself was also secretly desiring to be sent to Spain. And so, recognizing the certainty that no more than one of us has ever been transferred at a time, he persuaded our sadly gullible Inquisitor General to send me on that wild goose chase to the northern wilderness so that I would not be around when the emissary arrived, so that he would have the field clear for himself alone.

I have even come to believe that Fray Luis took on the case of the Dumb One specifically in an effort to embarrass me, to showcase the paucity of my achievement. Fray Luis gives not a hang about the Dumb One. Why else contrive to have his baptismal papers disappear except to humiliate me with the accusation that I'd not even bothered to check for them?

And now this covert threat regarding my ancestry, with all its implications of my unfitness! I would love to cry to the world, 'Fray Luis! He's the *Marrano!* But of course I have no proof of it.

This is a wicked world we live in. I should not even have to waste ink on such a trite observation, except that it is so painful to find the proof of it in the very high and Holy Office to which I've devoted my career.

I am praying all my assumptions are not so. I am praying further that Fray Luis has not already poisoned the emissary's mind against me, most lethally with this false *Marrano* business. And I have my counter-arguments prepared. Is it not so that Fray Luis did something rash and dishonest with the evidence in the case of the Dumb One? Is it not so that he seeds disharmony with scurrilous talk of his colleague's bloodlines? All this can be used against him. Or can it, if his accusation against me should prove true?

I want nothing more than to be out of this country. I want to sip fine, aged wines in Jerez.

As for the Dumb One, he dies tomorrow. It is both a terrible pity and sin that I must struggle to remind myself of this truth.

1 May

I awakened early, unable to sleep. I walked before dawn to the Plazuela del Volador. I can report that the *quemadero,* as prepared for this, its sole victim today, is maintained at a height of eight feet, yet its overall contours have been reduced, so that it is no more than twenty feet square, smaller even than the viewing stand. It has an air about it of expectancy, fresh fuel is piled up on it as if winter were coming. Already in the hours before sunrise, riffraff had begun to gather on the Plazuela, and hawkers were opening their stalls. Because of the scarcity of *relajados,* I am certain the crowd today will in no way compare to the monstrous one that came out for the grand Act of Faith last year. Indeed, the likelihood of only modest attendance, I'm sure, is what has determined the Inquisitor General to hold the ceremonial aspects of the day's proceedings inside the confines of the cathedral, out of the public traffic. It is commonplace, if the crowd is to be modest, to let it accumulate at that place of its most natural interest, namely, the place of burning, rather than let it appear even thinner by being divided between the site of the *Auto* and the site of the flames.

A cold mist hung in the air. The natives and *mestizos* that gathered in the grayness were nonetheless in a festive mood, eating their breakfasts of corn, gossiping, jostling for good positions from which to view the spectacle. I was in a dour mood myself, and I remain so. Nothing about this day has promise in it. I recall last year Fray Miguel de Castro, the perpetual optimist, trailing the last unrepentant one all the way to the Volador, in hope of hearing some last minute contrition. He will play that role of last confessor again today, but I spoke with him and he has spoken with the Dumb One, as of course have I, and even Fray Miguel de Castro holds out few hopes. 'A most persistent *negativo*,' is his analysis.

I had told myself that I would not attempt to see the Dumb One again. However, walking back from the Plazuela, I began to ask myself what good reason I had for this. Was it because I had said to him everything it was in my mortal power to say? Was it because I had already performed, by marrying them, the only human mercy that I could? Was it because his 'voice' in my mind had declared its own extinction?

I decided these reasons were inadequate, or in all events irrelevant, and in particular the question of the 'voice', which I had at last begun to classify as something of a myth, a wild, empathetic flight of my own imagination, even an indulgence on my own part of magic; or, even, the fatal charm of the Devil. For if it had been meant by God as a miracle to help me save the Dumb One's soul, it had surely failed. And if it had been meant by God to teach me the humility of failure, I knew in my guilty heart that it had also failed. And God does not fail in his will. I adjusted my way home in order to take me past the prison.

At the prison I was admitted and taken to the condemned's cell. His bride was not present. I was told she had been required to leave some quarter hour before, on account of the procedures necessary to be undertaken to prepare the Dumb One for his chosen fate. Fray Jorge used, even emphasized, that particular word 'chosen'. We were within the Dumb One's earshot at the time, and perhaps Fray Jorge meant to encourage him to see that his future was still essentially in his own hands. But I found the usage jarring. Had the Dumb One truly 'chosen' this?

He was being fitted with the habit of an impenitent. It was a standard habit in all respects, showing devils thrusting heretics into the flames of Hell. Similarly, the mitre he will wear is standard issue. More flames, more devils. There are moments when I wish we could commission one of our great artists, say, Diego Velasquez, to design us a more inspirational habit. On the Dumb One, it appeared, to my weary eyes anyway, more ludicrous than grave. Or is that the secret point?

With the bustle of those fitting him with his outfit, and Fray Jorge present to do the warden's duty of final prayers, there was an air of preoccupation in the Dumb One's cell, which fitted poorly with my presence. I felt only awkward and embarrassed. The Dumb One looked like an actor being made up. In a way, I despised him for it. Yet I waved his way, and he did wave back. He looked, perhaps, perplexed, even astounded. *How has it happened that I am here*, his expression seemed to say. And then, a rather distressing development. Fray Jorge's foot must have slid on the stone floor. He knelt to see what had caused it to slip. I watched him as his fingertips lifted the waxy residue of a candle from the floor. He asked the jailer, angrily, 'How was this permitted?'

'It was not, sir,' the jailer said.

'How is it here then?' Fray Jorge shouted. 'Today being

Sunday, yesterday being Saturday, the night before being the commencement of this wretched recalcitrant's sabbath…'

'The girl brought it! I saw it, sir! But I stomped it out, which is why you see only the candle remains in your hand.'

'The girl? What girl?'

'His bride, sir.'

Fray Jorge addressed the Dumb One, scorn and sarcasm equally in his voice. 'So you have a bride?'

The Dumb One said nothing.

Fray Jorge turned – I thought, oddly – to me. 'It's as I always say. When you see one rat, there are always more.'

I nodded tightly, not wanting an argument, and anxiously wondering if the 'more rats' was meant to include me. I soon left. I felt distressed, not only that the Dumb One was lighting his candle even unto his last sabbath on earth, but that he had brought the girl into it as well. Another soul in peril? And yet, was it not I who had facilitated it all? Was I not then a judaizer after all? The absurdity of all of it struck me.

On the way out, I passed Fray Miguel de Castro, who was on his way in. He shot me a grim glance. I felt suddenly light-headed, as if I were a part in an unimaginable farce.

I returned to my rooms, where I have written these notes and will now put on my own ceremonial robes, in time, I trust, or hope, *just* in time perhaps, to join the official procession. The official schedule for the day calls for its departure from the prison at seven o'clock, the *Auto de fe* in the cathedral from eight until ten o'clock, and the *quemadero* at noon.

Whatever else one might say about our Holy Office here, it has been, under our esteemed Inquisitor General, an office well-versed in detail, an office which gets things done on time. From dawn, our various officers and functionaries, as well as the secular representatives and their soldiers, gathered under our green and sable banner outside the prison walls. Promptly at seven, the Dumb One was brought forth from the dungeon, flanked by guards and trailed closely by Fray Miguel de Castro. The Dumb One's eyes swept here and there. Even more so than at his trial, he looked as if he could not quite believe that so many people should be gathered, even so many important people, at so early an hour, in robes and gowns, for himself alone. A one-man *Auto de Fe.* Not unprecedented, of course, but hardly the usual thing. I am not sure it has ever been calculated what effects such concentration of attention might have on the lone subject. Perhaps, I even dared hope, the Dumb One might be so impressed with our vast attention that he might feel in it Christ's underlying love, Christ's eternal concern, and so the sum of our massed bodies on this cool, damp morning might be the means of his salvation.

But it was not to be. He took his place behind the green and sable banner seemingly without heeding any of us, least of all Fray Miguel de Castro. I realized then, of course, who his scanning eyes had been searching for. Felicia, his bride, with his unborn child.

I followed his eyes until they steadied and focused, and then I found her myself, across the prison square, at as great a distance from any of us as she could be, as if we were the fright of God. She was wrapped in that humble scrap of blanket that had covered her from Monterrey to here. I could not see her face clearly at that distance, nor did I see her the moment she laid eyes on him, yet still what I thought I saw in her was shock, as if the sight of her beloved in that ridiculously tall mitre and sackcloth of crudely-drawn flames, reduced, as it were, to the part of universal jester, was the cruelest and saddest of revelations. Or perhaps I am only imputing to her a portion of my own feelings. I have seen many people in such humiliating garb and circumstances, but I have never seen one so alone.

Like all prisoners, the Dumb One had his hands tied in front of him, in which he held a rosary, a Bible and a candle. The irony of him being forced to carry a candle was not lost on me, though perhaps there were few others to appreciate it. Or, perhaps, I hoped, the Dumb One himself did. Something, one thing, for us to share.

Justitia et Misericordia, justice and mercy. Under this banner we marched, our parade of shame traversing the four blocks from prison to Zocalo and Cathedral in less than the allotted hour. Once in the Cathedral we assumed our customary places. I again sought the Dumb One's eyes, which now turned heavenward, apparently marveling at the high vaults and magnificent adornments. Our cathedral must surely have been the largest and most extraordinary building he had ever been in. Again I prayed that God's glory, inhabiting these stones, would similarly capture his heart. But the Dumb One gave no sign of it.

The mass and judgment, it was apparent, would be only moderately attended. Despite offers of spiritual benefits for attendance, the inhabitants of Mexico are well aware of the Archbishop's notorious long-windedness, particularly concerning matters of heresy. There has hardly been an *Auto* whose sails he has not sucked wind from by the tediousness and repetitiveness of his sermons. The Inquisitor General, it is rumored, has even spoken with him about this, but to no avail. And so the citizenry boycotts our Holy Service and takes its amusement instead at the *quemadero*. I blame them, of course, for voyeurism and vulgarity, but I blame us more, for failing to put on a decent show. In the meantime, while I fretted about the poor attendance, my eyes scanned the pews for the girl Felicia, whom I found, at last, not in a pew at all but standing in the left colonnade, as if a spy at the proceedings, as if she believed she did not belong here. I then searched for the *Suprema*'s emissary, Diego Hernando Montalves, whom I discovered taking his seat directly three rows before me, between representatives of the Viceroy and *Audiencia*. Fray Luis, I was relieved to observe, was no closer to him than I.

The mass was followed by the Archbishop's sermon, which I shall not waste paper on. Suffice it to say, he had it in for heretics, judaizers, Jews, Protestants, pagans, sinners, backsliders and common criminals. He was in favor of what we are all in favor of. He managed to impress these facts upon us in little more than an hour. I must say I felt pity for the Dumb One, that his last sermon should be this one. Would a better one have given him a better chance?

But then I began to critique my own pity, my constant fantasizing about the Dumb One's every 'chance'. Yes, he had had many chances, and taken none of them. That was the irreducible fact.

I thus found myself veering between two extremes, anger and a vast pity, as I watched the Dumb One, bewildered, like a caught unicorn, in his black-draped dock. I prayed for certainty in my thicket of doubt.

On conclusion of the sermon, the Inquisitor General and his fellow judges in the case stepped forward to state the verdict and sentence. They faced the front of the cross while the Dumb One faced the back of it, which has its symbolism, of course, but also the inevitable result that judges and judged stare at each other directly.

'Before pronouncing upon you, we call on you, Juan del Paso del Norte, one last time to repent and kiss the Cross and move yourself from eternal damnation to holy grace,' declared the Inquisitor General.

The Dumb One shook his head, his simple silence causing shivers of fear and shouts of rage to echo through the cathedral hall.

Then the Inquisitor General made the court's pronouncement: 'You, Juan del Paso del Norte, are found guilty of such pestilential and unrepented heresy that our Holy Office has determined you must be relaxed to the secular authority, to be dealt with in a stern and just manner as it sees fit, keeping in mind the blessed utterance of Jesus Christ our Savior as recorded by John, that "if a man abide not in me, he is cast forth as a branch, and is withered; and men gather them, and cast them into the fire, and they are burned." Thus saith the Lord, and thus saith this court.'

Soldiers again surrounded the Dumb One. The Cathedral was emptied, and our procession reformed on the Zocalo. The day had warmed. A glimmer of hazy sun poked through. And now the crowds had come out on the Zocalo, in numbers we could not have imagined inside the church. They were jeering and hissing the Dumb One, as crowds have always jeered and hissed the condemned, and the soldiers performed their rightful task more of preventing the Dumb One's immediate harm than his escape. In the meantime, the Inquisitor General must have been considerably relieved: his gamble on staging an Act of Faith for the Dumb One only, in hopes that it would remind the inhabitants of our majesty and authority and of how well we've swept the populace clean of contamination, appears to have earned a sufficient payoff, in the vulgar mob's jeering approval.

From here I shall abridge somewhat my writing of this day. I had wished to record the Dumb One's last moments and the circumstances of his condemnation, but I have less desire to record the details of his final demise. On the contrary, at the moment, I find something indelicate and even obscene in recalling those awful moments, as if by doing so I somehow align myself with the crowd's voyeurism. It is one thing to make public the fatal results of illicit and dangerous conduct, as a recitation and warning to others, but quite another to take pleasure in the reciting.

Nonetheless, a decent respect for the completeness of my enterprise exhorts me to record at least this much: When the Dumb One was brought to the *quemadero,* I still was hoping for a miracle. But I believed it would have to be a miracle. As he was brought to the stage, Fray Miguel de Castro even dismounted from the burro that had carried him from the Zocalo, in order for his ear to be close to the Dumb One's mouth, so that should God at the last give the Dumb One speech, he might hear any whisper. But there was no whisper, not of repentence nor anything else. The Dumb One's bride I could not see anywhere. From my own position on the viewing platform, I went from face to face in the sea of humanity that surrounded us, but could not find her. I resorted to my previous trick of following the Dumb One's eyes, but perhaps not even he could find her either. Where he did look, I looked, without result. Yet I was as certain as if I had been given an intimation of it that she was there.

From the moment the Dumb One was conveyed onto the *quemadero,* and so removed at last from the attendance of his last confessor, everything went expeditiously. Two soldiers led him to the post, where another lathered the exposed portions of his slender corpus with the oil and still a fourth secured him to the post. The only irregularity I observed was that while the mitre was taken from his head, the sackcloth was not removed from his body. I do not know if this was a novel gesture to modesty or an oversight. Between and over the heads of dignitaries seated in front of me, I attempted to catch glimpses throughout of the Dumb One's expression, and also, I must admit, whether his lips moved in silent contrition. I could see little that I dared categorize. His expression, indeed, seemed blank, as if he had been anesthetized, by some powerful drug or such. How could this be possible, I wondered, that he should go to his death with such equanimity? Or was the proper word for it courage? Or was the even more correct word dignity? I had never seen its like, and I have observed many *Autos*. And I wondered, further, how it could be that one who evidently did not believe in our Christian afterlife could make such a perfect example of his death? Was it only because his wife and his unborn child were his witnesses?

And then, the most terrible realization crystallized for me: we whose entire apparatus was designed to root out the insincere, were here punishing a man with death who, living, as he said, as if there is a God of love, had chosen sincerity over life itself. Here was a man dying for principle, and even now I was not sure what that principle was. Tears did not come to my eyes when I observed Diego Hernando Montalves, as our most distinguished visitor, do the honor of lighting the brand that would set the pyre aflame. Tears came to my eyes when I realized how little I knew this man I have called the Dumb One.

I had – indeed, I have now – only the vaguest outlines of him. A few clear acts, a 'voice' that was not a voice, a certain look, expressions, silence. Indeed, I re-read the pages of this journal for clues. But this journal itself, I fear, is as insubstantial as a cloud, when it comes to saying who this man among us was. A heretic, that is for sure. But what else? I could paint what I know of him in a thousand ways.

Dank clouds again covered up the sun, settling a chill over the Plazuela. Like a suitor eager with kisses, the flames leapt to the oil with which the Dumb One had been lathered. A fleeting sadness. Perhaps I saw a fleeting sadness. The same, if that's what it was, as when I first, by his cook fire, asked him about his beliefs. The flames soon reached as high as his eyes. I could not see where he was looking when they closed, but just as I was certain she was there, I was certain his eyes were on her. As I have written, I had reason to go back over the pages of this journal tonight. In doing so, I happened to observe my enthused and admiring descriptions of the grand *Auto* of last year. I am ashamed tonight of that enthusiasm. There is nothing to be excited about at the *quemadero*. If I learned one thing from the Dumb One today, it is that. Nor is there ecstasy to be sought in burning a man, as if the damned were consumed by something holy. I have long believed, and yet believe, that affliction may bring man closer to God, after the example of our Savior. But today I observed simply pain, in its every dimension and possibility, the unity of earthly pain and infernal pain. The cold dampness of the afternoon remains with me.

It was over in how long? From the moment Diego Hernando Montalves lit the brand to the moment there was so little left of him but ash and smoke that he could no longer be seen on the post? I might guess, perhaps fifteen minutes. The time, one might say, that we allotted. The time we talk about when we talk about such things. The time it might have taken the Dumb One himself to roast a delicious bit of pork on our campfire?

Enough. Even more than enough. May the Lord have mercy on his unconfessed soul.

1 May
later

It is almost midnight. Dear God, do You hear me? Dear God, have You abandoned me? Dear God, grant me some sign. Dear God, I will not state again my wretchedness, I will not state again my sinfulness, because I am not even capable of such statements, I am as an eternal liar, whose every word is but a shadow, no, a negation, of the truth it proclaims, I am in such a state that I might as well be that Dumb One who had no words at all, and yet dear God, it is Your pity, it is Your mercy, that I hear my lying voice beseech.

Fall dumb. Fall silent. Is it not more honorable? Was that the Dumb One's secret? I look and do not see You. I feel and do not feel You. You are not near. You are not in all that is in my world. Or have I simply lost the power to sense You? Am I deprived of grace? Is this what it feels like, to be deprived of grace?

Dear God, answer me, answer me soon, I pray, that I not perish.

Every thing, every object, my hand, my pen, this journal, the lamp, the bed, my books, the room, all stand alone, as if they stood for nothing more than themselves, as if they were not touched, as if they belonged to nothing else. Dear God, is this even possible? I am being punished. It must be that I am being punished.

The 'voice' came, and the 'voice' went, and took You with it. Dear God, is this even conceivable?

Was it my crime to cause him to burn? Or was it my crime to have doubts?

A word, any word.

That miraculous voice, that came and went like a spring breeze.

Who shall I ask forgiveness of?

Who shall hear a word I utter?

And what should it matter?

Lies and emptiness. Satan, be gone from me. Satan, Satan, a hundred times 'Satan', more lies, coming from my mouth, lies *because* they come from my mouth.

Is it because I am a *Marrano?* Is this the only truth that I can utter?

After the *Auto* this afternoon, I encountered Fray Sebastian. He thanked me for my stalwart testimony in the case against the Dumb One. 'We would have been lost without you.' 'I thought Fray Luis had us, but your resourcefulness saved the day.' He went on in that vein. I had always found Fray Sebastian an agreeable and trustworthy sort. Unprovoked, as if some oppressed precinct of my mind suddenly saw its chance for freedom, I found myself asking him if he had ever heard rumors of *Marrano* blood among the personnel of the Holy Office. 'What are you thinking?' he asked me.

Fray Sebastian, I would estimate, is seven or eight years my senior, he had already been here a decade when I arrived at the Holy Office, and in my early years particularly I often made confession to him. We were outside the refectory, in a much-frequented passageway to the common room, and I asked him to accompany me to one of the benches in the courtyard where there was no chance to be overheard. He did so without objection. I felt certain he must have some sense of my concern, but Fray Sebastian is a man of little revelatory expression (which helps explain, I believe, his outstanding success as a *promotor fiscal*).

Once we were seated by ourselves, with only the mockingbirds for our witness, I stated to him that a matter had arisen which I felt cast suspicion on another official of the Holy Office and thereby undermined our ability to function as a united and harmonious whole.

He asked me to elaborate.

I said, 'It is my belief, though I have no definite proof, that Fray Luis is prepared to spread the rumor that I am myself a *Marrano*.'

'Do you believe this rumor?'

'Of course I do not.'

'Who has the rumor gone to?'

'I only know that I received an anonymous note.'

'Why do you suspect Fray Luis?'

'Because the note appeared immediately after my testimony embarrassed him at trial. And because Fray Luis has long condescended to me, and considers me a rival, and wishes the *Suprema*'s emissary to choose him for a Spanish transfer over myself.'

'Did you investigate whether the note might contain truth?'

'I did not. I had my suspicion that something in my deposition concerning the ancestries of the Dumb One and myself might have contained a kernel of something that inspired Fray Luis to embellish if not outright lie. But I feared that if I then conducted archival research, Fray Luis would observe this and use it as proof of my "guilty conscience". But no one has ever before given me the smallest reason to think it is so.'

Fray Sebastian's customary impassivity softened somewhat. He seemed, indeed, sympathetic to my case. He pursed his lips and I felt that his mild eyes slightly smiled. 'What did the note say, precisely, Fray Alonso?'

'"Does it not take one *Marrano* to know another?" Plainly referencing the case of the Dumb One and my identification of him.'

'Yes. It is so.'

'What is "so"? What I say?'

'What you say, of course. But also… what "Fray Luis" says. Oh, not literally, of course. I wouldn't become hysterical, Fray Alonso. There are plenty of inquisitors who have had some ancestor or other they would rather not have heard of.'

'What are you saying, Fray Sebastian?' My mouth lost its saliva. Even my eyesight seemed to dim, as if the light of the afternoon fled from them.

'Only, Fray Alonso, that I am pleased to say it's your blessed day. It was not Fray Luis who uncovered this truth about your forebear Don Federico de la Ronda, it was I. Only by doing my due diligence, of course, wishing to give our accused, despite your impressive deposition, every opportunity that justice might allow. I checked every claim in your deposition, which brought me inevitably, I'm afraid, to Volume Six of *Proceedings and Sessions of the Holy Office* where I found that the accused's ancestor Don Tomas Rodrigues de Santangel was indeed a New Christian suspected, but never proved, of having judaizing secrets. And I will confess my curiosity got the better of me, given the rather astounding number of suspects there were amongst the early conquistadors, and my eyes wandered only a page or two before they discovered that your own ancestor was in precisely the same category. A New Christian, a convert, without a doubt. Suspected but never proved of being a secret Jew.'

'Then… then I am a fraud.'

'Really, you are less of a fraud than you were. Does not knowledge set us free? Does it not bring us closer to God? I only brought it to your attention to help you, Fray Alonso. Better you know it now than someday it be brought against you unawares by the likes of Fray Luis. Better you understand how it shapes your faith. Your "secret", if that's how you wish it, is safe with me. I only chose anonymity because I felt it would have been better for you to make the actual discovery yourself. I hadn't counted on your mistrust of Fray Luis getting in the way of your own research.'

He then cited chapter and verse, that is to say, the page and line numbers where my ancestor's name appears, bade me a cordial adieu, and arose and left me alone in the courtyard.

THE MARRANO

entries from 2 May to 5 May 1650

2 May

Nothing. Nothing to report. Nothing to sense.

I have drawn my curtain. A candle lights my darkness.

I shall not pray until my prayer is not a lie.

And yet, if the foundation of my faith was Your nearness, the intimation of You in all that is, even to the bosom of Your Holy Church and its teachings and wisdom and practice, then had my faith too easy a path? With so many signs, with such assurance, what was left for faith but a little leap?

Now there is an abyss. A chasm of unknown, perhaps infinite, dimension. Shall I leap *this*? Am I not afraid?

When there is nothing, when there is only darkness, when but a single candle is lit, there, *there* is a test of faith. When there is nothing else *but* faith, when faith is… what?

This single candle?

How infinitely greater was the challenge to the Dumb One's

faith than to my own. Or is not his challenge now mine?

I write, but to whom? Do I dare to say 'to Whom?'

'Dear God.' 'Heavenly Father.' 'Lord and Savior.' 'You.' I shall not utter names until the names are not lies in my teeth.

I do not sense the eternal possibilities.

Why should I leap? Even if I were not afraid... Even if I were not enraged... Even if I were not ashamed...

I am alone.

3 May

And yet today I went about my life, because what else was there to do? To live as if I were Fray Alonso. Now there was a job, there was a calling! To find irony in truth's place. To be a ghost in the corridors of the world.

And indeed, I soon discovered, if I were going to live as if I were Fray Alonso and nothing more nor less, as everything in the world was nothing more nor less, then it would not be so bad a thing to be transferred to Spain. A bit of wine, wondrous monuments, new landscapes. Why not?

The foregoing thoughts being occasioned by an invitation to dine with Diego Hernando Montalves which I received early this morning. I would abandon my darkness, so to speak, in search of worldly possibility.

The invitation was not for myself alone. Also present at lunch were the Inquisitor General, Fray Sebastian, and Fray Miguel de Castro. Fray Luis was not there, from which I inferred that his lunch two days ago with the emissary was merely coincidental, having to do with the I.G. wishing to arrange a succession of meals whereby we all might be able to meet the distinguished guest.

I would say that the lunch, from the outset, was an opportunity for me to see other human beings stripped away, without, as it were, the devils and angels on their shoulders. Plain men, stout or gaunt, greedy or austere, nor could I tell one thing for certain about them, even whether they were utterly weightless and might fly up to the sky at any minute or whether they were so weighted down with a matter infinitely dense that they might sink into the earth. I am a fool, I am ignorant of this world. And I always have been.

It was an occasion for the *Suprema*'s envoy to impress upon us that he was a man with 'new views'. He expressed to us at length, and with various reiterations of the theme, that a certain kind of overzealousness, unhinged from careful consideration, might be doing the mission of our Holy Office more harm than good. If not for my inward haughty indifference, I might privately have bridled at what was obviously Diego Hernando Montalves' touting of the political over the ethical and theological. In the event, I held my peace, not without calculating that I had more immediate and personal matters to raise with him.

When we finally rose from the table, where my appetite was oddly considerable, I approached Diego Hernando Montalves directly and told him what a brave and well-considered and appropriate talk I thought he had given us. No amount of flattery felt beyond me at the moment and he thanked me for my kind words.

Then he said, 'It was you, wasn't it, who brought the case against this miserable heretic relaxed yesterday?'

'It was,' I said.

'I commend your zeal,' he said, which might have sounded complimentary in another context, but which I understood, from his words at table, were anything but.

'Well really, I was only doing what I was asked, by the Inquisitor General,' I said.

Unfortunately the I.G. was within range to hear us, and he put in, 'Because you were the only man for the job, Fray Alonso!'

'Thank you, sir,' I said, because what else could I say?

'Fray Alonso here is a tough old nut,' the I.G. continued. 'If you were a heretic, you wouldn't want him to know about it.' And he went on, quite inevitably, to explain how the case against the heretic of yesterday would have been lost except for my exceptional testimony, including my own journal writings, which I brought to bear at the last instant against him.

Again I was forced to thank the Inquisitor General for being colossally unhelpful to my current hopes.

Out of nausea for hearing my own unctuous words, and in determination to get them all out of my mouth as soon as possible before I should become actually sick, I hazarded a change of subject. 'What I wished to discuss with you, Don Diego, is a matter of transfer. I don't know if this is the appropriate moment, perhaps it would be best, if you had a few minutes, for us to sit down and perhaps I could impress upon you my thoughts. But since I am not sure how long you will be gracing us with your presence, I thought I should at least bring the matter to your attention now.'

'What sort of transfer are you thinking about, Fray Alonso?' he asked.

'To Spain, actually, sir. I have been, as the Inquisitor General can tell you, a functionary of this Office for thirteen years, and I am indeed a native of this place, but I feel that a transfer to the Peninsula, provided I committed myself to returning to New Spain once my term elapsed, would be beneficial not only to myself, in terms of perhaps sharpening the tools I bring to my job here, but to our Holy Office in Mexico itself, which ever benefits from inputs from across the ocean. I am sure, for instance, that the concerns you expressed at dinner today would find a second voice in my own, if I had the opportunity to absorb the *Suprema*'s new views directly for a period of time.'

I might have gone on in that vein, uttering whole paragraphs that careened in my mind like so many empty boxes, but the envoy halted me there. 'Fray Alonso, pray let me interrupt you a moment. I don't want you to waste needless words. But you know it's been our policy to transfer only one man from an overseas Office at any given time.'

'I do know that. Indeed, it's precisely why I am approaching you now.'

'But Fray Luis is going,' the Inquisitor General put in. 'I thought you knew that.'

... And so... and so. I concede defeat. Even cheerfully. I concede cheerfully to being outmaneuvered by half. I concede cheerfully, even, that Diego Hernando Montalves with his 'new views' and Fray Luis with his, are probably a match made in heavenly spheres. Chapter closed, ha-ha, ha-ha. But why did I not guess the ending long before now?

I returned to my room, vomited copiously, and commenced to write this record.

4 May

Fray Jorge delivered to me today a note found in the Dumb One's cell. It was folded until it was little more than a wad, but my name, in the crude, boxy letters of the half-literate, was written on the face of it.

I thanked Fray Jorge. He told me that he was still 'determined to get to the bottom of the matter' regarding the delivery of the last candle to the Dumb One. Eager for him to leave, I nodded sympathetically, wishing not to get into an argument with him. As soon as he was gone, I undid the several folds of the paper.

I was certain Fray Jorge believed the Dumb One had written these words. I was equally certain the Dumb One was incapable of doing so.

The note said only this: 'Fray Alonso. You were kind to me. I forgive you. Juan del Paso del Norte.'

A most curious and awful sense took hold of me on reading these square, half-formed words. *If I were him, would I forgive me?* The unmistakable love that I had ever felt when I contemplated the name or image or idea of our Savior, that unmistakable, all-embracing, palpable love which had always been the surest guarantor of my faith… that same love, so wretchedly lost, I felt emanating from the scrap of paper in my hand. It felt, moreover, uncannily as if the Dumb One's 'voice' had returned to my mind for one last visit.

And when I then, in urgent comparison, brought to my mind the images of the Inquisitor General and Fray Luis and Fray Jorge and even Fray Sebastian and the *Suprema* and its emissary, indeed all the appurtenances and representatives of our Holy Office rolled up into a heap in my mind, I found no such love.

Has Satan finally found me out? Or have I been, miraculously, reborn?

My mind and my heart are at war, and not even one against the other, but in utter upheaval, mind against mind, heart against heart, all against all.

I who anyway thought he had lost his heart, when he lost everything else.

That name, which the tribunal named him. *Juan del Paso del Norte.* Did he have a family name? I never knew it.

The Inquisitor General invited me to his office this morning. He was in an expansive mood, and offered me a cup of chocolate, which since the arrival of his cook from the south has become the I.G.'s tonic of choice.

I had no idea why he had summoned me. I was poorly slept. The chocolate seemed to make me only more drowsy, so that when he said to me, 'Here, here, Fray Alonso. There may be some chance for you yet,' I was not quite prepared.

'Chance? In what regard?' I asked.

'Have you forgotten your desire so quickly? I had a discussion with the envoy. We agreed that he might have been too hasty the other day.'

'Too hasty in what, sir?'

'This whole business of rules and precedents. After all, why should it be, it's not as if God commanded it, that we should ship only one man back to Spain at a time? Things have been quiet here. We're not exactly overflowing with business. Anyway, it's no sure thing by any means. I would say the odds are no better than half. But Diego Hernando Montalves has agreed to meet with you.'

'About my going to Spain, sir?'

'My, you're a dullard this morning. You'll have to be more on the ball than this, if you expect to impress the envoy. He'll see you tomorrow at four.'

'Thank you, sir. This is stunning news,' I said.

'Oh, and one other thing. I'd just like you to be aware of it. You wouldn't know where that whore who visited your Dumb One is abiding, would you? Fray Jorge has decided to make an example of her, and I must say that I agree. We can't have judaizing right on our own premises. Moreover, we have to be seen to be doing *some*thing, or they'll cut my budget altogether.'

'So you're considering a *clamosa* against this woman?'

'If we can find the whore. I've put Fray Luis in charge.'

'But I thought he was leaving.'

'This should be a fast one. Open-and-shut, wouldn't you think?'

'I think... what I think... Sir, is this not precisely the sort of excessive zeal that our respected visitor has been warning us against?'

'Oh, yes, of course. You know, he talks a good game. But when it comes to determining budget, they still want results, they want to see cases on the schedule. You know what sort of cut they are talking about? Twenty-five percent. I said to him, I cannot maintain my staff with a twenty-five percent cut.'

'So if I were sent to Spain, I would be part of your fiscal solution,' I said.

'You could think about it that way. A lucky break for both of us, no?'

'Yes. Certainly.'

'But we definitely need your help with this judaizing whore. Didn't you find lodgings for her? Fray Jorge thought so.'

'I did. But that was days ago.'

'Well just give the address to Fray Luis.'

'With all due respect, sir, Fray Luis... created much harsh feeling. If it is he who goes for her...'

'Who gives a hang what feelings that whore has, she *should* have harsh feelings...'

'I wasn't so much thinking of her, sir. If we go into a public tavern, and a scene results, you know it can only look bad for the Office, manhandling a woman, all of that. It is a matter of maintaining public support, sir.'

'So you want to go get her? Fine. Be my guest. I will tell Fray Luis.'

'I'm not sure she'll still be found in the city, sir,' I said. 'But I will do my best.'

'Go to it, then. And I'll tell Diego Hernando Montalves to be expecting you tomorrow at four.'

'Thank you, sir.'

'And if I could suggest, Fray Alonso... Don't bore him with your theories of how the Office has gone soft. He will not be interested.'

'Of course not, sir.'

And so I left.

I returned to my rooms, where I immediately began to record this conversation with the Inquisitor General.

I am still in utter turmoil. No, if possible, I am in greater turmoil. Ah, gorgeous, civilized, brilliant Spain, land of my dreams!

I am in the utmost turmoil, yet I know what I shall do next.

5 May
later

I did indeed find Felicia. She was still at the very tavern where I had delivered her on the night she came to my rooms. As they had discerned she had no money, and apparently was not willing to whore herself, they had put her out with the chickens. Dirty straw was her resting place. Yet her face was scrubbed. She gave the appearance of one who has no idea what the next minute or hour will bring. She owed money, she had nothing to eat but garbage, she had only her body and what she bore in her womb. I told her the danger she was in. I bade her come with me. She would not at first, because of her debt to the tavern keeper. I paid that debt for her, and we then went through the city together. At every turn I feared being watched and followed. I had gone alone to fetch her, which by itself could raise suspicions. If Fray Luis, or even Fray Jorge, had seen me depart without a standard detachment, what dark assumptions might they leap to?

I asked Felicia if she wished to return to Monterrey. She said she wished only to go to the place that she and the Dumb One had thought of going to, she wished to go to *Alto California*. I asked her why she would wish to go to a place which, from the little I had ever heard, is more barren and desolate than even that miserable settlement where I first discovered the Dumb One. She said a client had once told her about it, that it was where you could be alone, a place of freedom, and she had told the Dumb One and he had nodded and smiled. I could not argue with a dead man's smile, least of all her dead husband's, but I did wonder what her client was likely to have told her, in their sordid ten minutes together. She had not the smallest idea how to get to *Alto California*, nor even where it was, except that it was beside a sea. I told her few men went there, and fewer women, and the journey would be difficult and perilous; further, that I had not even heard of an overland trail but that there might be a boat from Santa Lucia; but even the journey over the mountains to Santa Lucia would not be without danger. Of course, I was speaking to one who had made her way from Monterrey, a distance several times greater. And, having nothing, she could not be deterred by the thought of loss.

Nor did I have a better idea to suggest, with Fray Luis and the others soon enough to be after her, if they were not already. I could delay them, perhaps, by reporting that I had not yet found her, but after that they would resort to their own devices and the city would not be safe for her.

I gave her all the money I had on my person. I accompanied her, with continuing caution and apprehension, to a corner of the Zocalo where I understood that journeys to Santa Lucia, as well as to Veracruz, Monterrey and destinations to the north and south, were organized. A train had just departed for Santa Lucia at daybreak. Felicia said she would walk quickly and catch up to it. On my honor as an official of the Holy Office – since I had already emptied my pockets – I engaged a carriage and we drove together to the start of the Santa Lucia road, where she stepped out. I stepped out with her. I offered to drive her a further distance, so that she would have a better chance to catch up with the mule train. She declined, then she thanked me, and I saw that her eyes were averted. She again seemed like the frail waif who had arrived at my door not many nights previous. I asked her: 'Felicia, was it you who wrote the note where Juan forgave me? Not that it matters. But I never believed that Juan could write letters.' She continued to eye the ground. I knew that what I suspected must be so. I watched her set off and grow distant from me, until she was a speck on the road. She was like someone who had put herself entirely in the care of the horizon.

6 May

Am I being watched? Is my every move being scrutinized? Have traps been set? Have I already failed some test?

I stay in my room. This morning I went to the Inquisitor General and reported the 'whore's' disappearance. Was I credible? Did some secret part of me flinch? The Inquisitor General performs a bureaucrat's role now, but there was a time when he could ferret out a soul's faintest doubt. This morning I could feel his scorn. After I told him my disappointing news – *only* after I told him my disappointing news – he informed me, as if it were a casual irrelevance he only just remembered, 'Oh, Diego Hernando Montalves is indisposed today. He'll have to reschedule you. You will be informed.'

So I did not play their game, and they will not play mine. This much I know.

I must leave. Now.

And would it not be altogether better if I ceased writing in this journal, if I turned it into ashes forthwith? This journal that convicted the Dumb One could as easily now convict me.

Yet, most strangely, I have a powerful urge to write more, not less.

You want a confession? I'll give you a confession! Every man or woman I condemned, and some I only dream of, dance in the forefront of my mind like accusing ghosts. *Marranos*, souls called pigs for failing to believe – yet it is the things they *did* believe that haunt me now. Once I heard the Dumb One's 'voice' and felt a companion in this world. Now my own lonely mind calls forth all these others, their testimonies, their evidence, their defenses, as if a cacophony from Heaven or Hell. Against what? Against *me!* I could write a hundred tales, I would not even have to consult the archives. But I have not pages, and I have not time.

Tomorrow they will pursue me. Tomorrow, if not tonight, they will know I helped the girl's escape. I will not be going to Spain. I laugh like a *Marrano*, bitterly, to think of it.

Was this finally the purpose of the Dumb One's 'voice', was this its miracle, that I should come to know the sufferings of others even as I come to know some paltry yet precious thing about myself?

6 May
again

Or is it rather his revenge, that my mind whirls in the constant bedlam of their wretched pleas?
    Lord, I pray a moment's peace.

6 May
again

And has the old, old question lost its sting? Who is talking, God or Satan, Satan or God?
    Is it not pathetic that, after all, I seem, like all the other wretches of the earth, to fear for my mortal life?

23 June
Santa Lucia

I made my departure. I traveled alone over the mountains. From the peaks I could see the trail two days in each direction. I never saw Felicia ahead of me, nor trailing me a standard detachment. Those shadow men who used to be my own. Their dark robes. Now I wear the blankets of the native. My disguise.

Ha! As if a standard detachment would not know the Office Historian!

But I am here now. I have bought passage aboard the *Santa Barbara*, which is in truth little more than a coaster, a modest fishing vessel with brave hopes. But I have met her captain, Captain Lopez, and he seems an amiable and capable man. I am not averse to putting my fate in his hands. His brother commands a like vessel, and it appears it was on this other ship, which departed ten days ago, that Felicia embarked. I had resolved to gift her with this journal. Not for her, but for the Dumb One's posterity. So they might see the madness of the world, and pray for their own escape from it.

For my own part, I have heard the most dispiriting tales of the deserts of *Alto California*, but I put them in fresh perspective. Did not the great men of our Holy Church, in the days before it was corrupted, seek out the hottest and most desolate places in order to become nearer to God? They abandoned everything rich and easy and populated, and so shall I. I shall be, even, perhaps, like the Dumb One, who also wandered a desert. To live as if there is a loving God. Is this the ethic of the lost man, or the only hope for man?

I declare today: wherever Christ is, He is not in Our Holy Office.

My own little heresy, continued.

Love and affliction. Affliction and love. I begin to know the one. Will it lead me toward the other?

Last night in this decrepit inn where I had been informed that

Felicia stayed before me, I took a knife from table to my room and with it performed that bloody act which marks a man in the book of life or in the book of death.

A matter of some dispute. It depends, it seems, on who you ask. In all events I did it. A circumcised Christian: what name will they call me now? Call it a gesture to my friend, or call it what you will. Today I confess to my nether parts being in some considerable pain. Santa Lucia is not a settlement where balms and unguents are in plentiful supply.

24 June
aboard Santa Barbara

This morning, in Santa Lucia's modest plaza, where anyone might recognize anyone, I observed three men in dark robes. One of these I believe I recognized, but I was so quick to bury my face in my blankets and pursue another direction that I could not be sure.

Now I am aboard ship, but we have yet to embark. It appears that it will be two hours more. Captain Lopez barks orders, his sailors scurry about. Securing ropes, repairing sails, boarding supplies. There is nothing to be done about it, even if I had money to bribe, which I do not. The world must do its work.

I refuse to secrete myself in the hold. I choose not to write my last entry, if it shall be this, in dankness and fear. And what would it profit, anyway? If the standard detachment comes aboard, is it conceivable they will not search for me in every nook and cranny? No, the sun is shining. A new day perhaps awaits. Our prow is pointed towards *Alto California*. I will arrive there or not.

Against the more adverse of possibilities, I shall now deposit this journal in some unlikely place.

Only this wish of mine remains to be recorded: that in the event I perish in fire or at sea, a stranger may find this like a bottle on the shore and do with it as I would have done had I lived, namely, before retreating to the solitude which is the single thread remaining of my hopes for my own wicked soul, to seek out in the deserts or encampments of our northern destination that modest woman of Monterrey named Felicia, the mother of the child of someone I once knew, and hand this book to her, so the generations to come of this someone I once knew may know his story.

Peaks Island Branch Library
129 Island Avenue
Peaks Island, ME   04108